BYRNE

Born in Manchester in 1917, Anthony Burgess was edu-
cated at the Xaverian College in the city and at Manchester
University, of which he held a doctorate. He served in the
army from 1940 to 1956, and as a colonial education offi-
cer in Malaya and Borneo from 1954 to 1960, in which
year, as he put it, 'his brief but irreversible unemployability
having been decreed by a medical death sentence, he
decided to try to live by writing'. His output comprises over
fifty books. He was a Visiting Fellow of Princeton University and a Distinguished Professor of City College, New
York. He was created a Commandeur des Arts et des Lettres
by the French President and a Commandeur de Merite
Culturel by Prince Rainier of Monaco. Anthony Burgess
died in 1993.

BY ANTHONY BURGESS

NOVELS

The Long Day Wanes:
    Time For A Tiger
    The Enemy In The Blanket
    Beds In The East
The Right To An Answer
The Doctor Is Sick
The Worm And The Ring
Devil Of A State
One Hand Clapping
A Clockwork Orange
The Wanting Seed
Honey For The Bears
Inside Mr Enderby
Nothing Like The Sun: A Story
    Of Shakespeare's Love-Life
The Eve Of Saint Venus
The Vision Of Battlements
Tremor Of Intent
Enderby Outside
MF
Napoleon Symphony
The Clockwork Testament; Or,
    Enderby's End
Beard's Roman Women
Abba Abba
Man Of Nazareth
1985
Earthly Powers
The End Of The World News
Enderby's Dark Lady
The Kingdom Of The Wicked
The Pianoplayers
Any Old Iron
The Devil's Mode (short stories)
A Dead Man In Deptford
Byrne

AUTOBIOGRAHY

Little Wilson And Big God
You've Had Your Time

FOR CHILDREN

A Long Trip To Teatime
The Land Where The Ice Cream
    Grows

THEATRE

Oberon Old And New
Blooms Of Dublin

VERSE

Moses

NON FICTION

English Literature: A Survey For
    Students
They Wrote In English
    (for Italian schools)
Language Made Plain
Here Comes Everybody: An
    Introduction To James Joyce
    For The Ordinary Reader
The Novel Now: A Student's
    Guide To Contemporary Fic-
    tion
Urgent Copy: Literary Studies
Shakespeare
Joysprick: An Introduction To
    The Language Of James Joyce
New York
Hemingway And His World
On Going To Bed
This Man And Music
Homage To Quert Yuiop
A Mouthful Of Air

TRANSLATION

The New Aristocrats
The Olive Trees Of Justice
The Man Who Robbed Poor
    Boxes
Cyrano de Bergerac
Oedipus The King

EDITOR

A Shorter Finnegan's Wake

Anthony Burgess

BYRNE

VINTAGE

Published by Vintage 1996

2 4 6 8 10 9 7 5 3 1

First published in Great Britain by
Hutchinson, 1995

Vintage
Random House, 20 Vauxhall Bridge Road,
London SW1V 2SA

Random House Australia (Pty) Limited
20 Alfred Street, Milsons Point, Sydney
New South Wales 2061, Australia

Random House New Zealand Limited
18 Poland Road, Glenfield,
Auckland 10, New Zealand

Random House South Africa (Pty) Limited
PO Box 2263, Rosebank 2121, South Africa

Random House UK Limited Reg. No. 954009

A CIP catalogue record for this book
is available from the British Library

ISBN 0 09 959301 7

Papers used by Random House UK Ltd are natural, recyclable products made from wood grown in sustainable forests. The manufacturing processes conform to the environmental regulations of the country of origin

Printed and bound in Great Britain by
Cox & Wyman, Reading, Berkshire

To you and you and you.
Also you.

'Prudence, prudence,' the pigeons call,
'Scorpions lurk   the gilded meadow,
An eye is embossed on the island wall.
The running tap casts a static shadow.'

'Caution, caution,' the rooks proclaim,
'The dear departed, the weeping widow,
Will meet in you in the core of flame.
The running tap casts a static shadow.'

'Act, act!' the ducks give voice.
'Enjoy the widow in the meadow.
Drain the sacrament of choice.
The running tap casts a static shadow.'

F.X.E.

CONTENTS

Part One   3

Part Two   45

Part Three   85

Part Four   103

Part Five   133

Byrne

a novel

Anthony Burgess

ONE

ONE

Somebody had to do it. Blasted Byrne
Pulled out a bunch of dollars from his pocket,
Escudos, francs and dirhams. 'Let them learn
If they've a speck of talent not to mock it
But plant it and expect a slow return.
I whizzed mine skywards like a bloody rocket.
Tell what they call a cautionary tale.
Here's on the nail. Expect more in the mail.'

He thought he was a kind of living myth
And hence deserving of *ottava rima*,
The scheme that Ariosto juggled with,
Apt for a lecherous defective dreamer.
He'd have preferred a stronger-muscled smith,
Anvilling rhymes amid poetic steam, a
Sort of Lord Byron. Byron was long dead.
This poetaster had to do instead.

Some lines attributed to Homer speak
Of someone called Margites. 'Him the gods
Had not made skilled in craft or good in Greek.
He failed in every art.' Against the odds
His name survives. His case is not unique.
He should lie with forgotten odds and sods,
But still he serves to nominate a species
And lives while Byrne is mixed with his own faeces.

Byrne's name survives among film-music-makers
Because the late-night shows subsist on trash.
His opera's buried by art's undertakers,
His paintings join his funerary ash.
He left no land. 'My property's two achers,'
Stroking laborious ballocks. As for cash,
He lived on women, paying in about
Ten inches. We don't know what they paid out.

Handsome enough, there was no doubt of that –
Blue-eyed and with an Irish peasant's stature,
His belly flat, it never ran to fat;
Possessed of quite a punch whose crack could match your
Boundary-winning slam; lithe as a cat,
With two great paws, a natural outfield catcher;
Not that he ever wasted time on sport
Save only for the amatory sort.

The Irish are peculiar, no doubt:
They prefer drink to women. Nightly splurges
On whiskey, pints of plain or creaming stout
Serve to inhibit their erotic urges.
Seed-spending's peccative, but seed will out,
As Dr Kettle said. The Irish clergy's
At one with booze in locking semen in,
Though holy wedlock will annul the sin.

Byrne was no Rechabite by any means;
Drink was for him an aphrodisiac.
A foreign substance in the family genes
Burned up this Byrne alone. Long ages back,
When restive Erin was a redhaired queen's
Pain in the arse, the Spanish took a crack
At heretic England with their proud Armada,
Striking her navy hard, but that struck harder.

6

God's wind blew and they scattered, and some scattered
To Ireland's coast. When they had dried their doublets,
Survival seemed the only thing that mattered.
They swilled their buttermilk from peasant goblets
And, vowing they would never more be battered
By wind and wave, said, with a Spanish sob, 'Let's
Resign ourselves to pigshit, peat and mud,
And tickle these mad Irish with our blood.'

The Spaniard darkly shone from Byrne's complexion,
Though this was tempered by his mother's colour.
She was a Liverpudlian confection,
With Wales and Glasgow brightening the duller
Pallor, and a half-hazy recollection
Of sourmilk skin upon a Nordic skull, a
Tobacco-chewer's beard, half-grey, half-flaxen,
Proclaiming Dutch or Dane or Swede or Saxon.

Since Ireland was all England's, Irish reason
Said England was all Ireland's, and it showed
In July barbering or, at any season,
Setting down rails or mammocking the road.
O'Connell preached his demagogic treason:
The English harrow crushed the Irish toad;
Freed, though not freed of economic panics,
Ireland would not use England as an annexe.

The County Mayo Byrnes were not political:
They only wanted to be free to eat.
Their situation wobbled to the critical
Each harvest time. Pigs were forbidden meat
That paid the farm-rent to the parasitical
Absentee landlord. Over smoky peat
They munched their murphies, stirred their rancid stirabout.
Poverty was the one thing to confer about.

Old Peter Byrne could not say: 'This is my land.'
So when the blight killed the potato crop,
He spat upon the stones, then cursed awhile and
Announced that Liverpool was their next stop,
A Celtic port in John Bull's primary island,
Where other Byrnes already ran a shop
That catered to the poor's nutritive needs
By selling wormy cabbages and swedes.

The vegetable Byrnes sent off the fare,
And then the seasick vegetableless,
Hearing the Cunard sirens blast the air,
Settled to chronic urban shiftlessness,
Except for Kate, who, with a dancing flair,
Cavorted at the Empire in undress
And fired the fancy of a cotton broker.
Her brother Pat became a Cunard stoker.

Another brother came like Christmas sun
When Byrne the father thought his wells were dry.
His wife's fertility had months to run
Before the menopause should bid it fly.
It seemed to him that what the Lord had done
Was like the dayspring flashing from on high.
His knowledge of the Bible being dim,
He did not think of Ann and Joachim.

It was coincidence that made them christen
The fruit of this late coupling Sean or John.
Paternal pride made rheumy optics glisten
Behind the mended glasses they had on.
It brought the country past alive to listen
To lullabies culled from a time long gone.
But, like Saint Joseph, he'd a certain doubt
About his wife the nights that he was out.

She was a pretty woman, with a figure
Whose slimness was a fruit of malnutrition.
Her eyes were like a doe's, though rather bigger
Because her face bespoke her past condition.
Was someone tupping her with cash and vigour?
She spread a table rich for the position
Of a mere Mersey Harbour Board nightwatchman.
The swine, he thought, could hardly be a Scotchman.

But Father Leary brooked no contradiction
About the unitary fatherhood.
Paternity was but a legal fiction,
And God was good, particularly good,
As was made clear from scriptural depiction,
At fertilising. Earthly fathers stood
Stuck in a kind of foster-parent's groove:
True fatherhood's a thing you cannot prove.

Catholic, of course, and good as Catholics went,
She crossed herself at thunder and forked lightning.
Hearing the sacring bell, she duly bent,
Ate fish on Fridays and went in for tightening
Her corset by eschewing stout in Lent.
The hellfire doctrine she found rather frightening,
But didn't fancy hymning the Almighty
Paraded in a chilly cotton nighty.

Young John grew up a pagan like his dad,
Even more pagan when his dad was dead.
The Christian Brothers schooling that he had
Assailed his rump but passed beyond his head.
His sister was, though long gone to the bad,
Good at odd hand-outs, so his mother said.
Pat stoked away and sent home half his screw.
They managed: Merseysiders sometimes do.

John had a treble voice so sweetly piercing
It quite belied his boyish heathen heart.
Old ladies, when they heard the little dear sing,
Could not forbear to let the teardrops smart.
He got a great audition. They said: 'Here, sing
This *Agnus Dei* – see, the solo part.'
And that was in the massive polyhedral
Holy of holies, Liverpool Cathedral.

He sang and sang, inspiring holy love,
But not averse to dirtying his hassock,
And then he'd give another lad a shove,
Who would shove back, being no Sacher-Masoch.
Then, after rendering 'Wings of a Dove',
He'd wipe his snotty snout upon his cassock.
The Choirmaster did not appear to mind,
But he was growing deaf as well as blind.

During his sweetly vocal pre-pubescence,
John got a post that could be termed sub-clerical.
A shipping firm paid for his daily presence
Dogsbodying. And now the youthful lyrical
Gift had to go. To mock his adolescence,
The larynx squeaked or boomed. But, by a miracle,
Singing, while tidying his master's desk,
He found he'd turned into a young de Reszke.

Well, not quite of that heavy smoker's metal.
Say John McCormack, who became a papal
Count, gifted with a mistier, milder fettle,
Or syrupy, like drippings from the maple,
Or sensuous-soft, like stroking a rose-petal,
Whose songs would be the repertorial staple
Of Irish airs or such innocuous salads
As bland recitals of Victorian ballads.

John had, in fact, one of those tenor voices
You only find among the sons of Erin,
A sugary warbling flute just like James Joyce's,
Whose talent didn't get him anywhere in
The singing business. Still, he had two choices:
Butchering English was his other care. In
All honesty I'll give my verdict. This is:
He should have sung and not spewed up *Ulysses*.

John Byrne, not John McCormack, couldn't write,
Except fair copies of the company's letters,
But he would take his voice out every night
In temporary remission from the fetters
Of clerkly slavery. In the smoky light
Of pub or club or parish hall he'd get a s-
-Mall recompense for singing out his soul
In Tom Moore's words, set to the tunes he stole.

One Christmas he sang solo in *Messiah* —
With 'Comfort ye, my pee-eople' etcetera.
He saw a dark-haired mezzo in the choir,
And a few days after he'd properly met her a
Fleshly affection in them both took fire.
They kissed and colled in parks and fields and, better, a
Warm bed, her own. There's danger, I suppose,
In singing sacred oratorios.

Here name was Sybil (Delphic prophetess:
The etymology meant nothing to her).
She was the sort of girl whose comeliness
Lies less in shape than sensual allure.
There are such women, often drab in dress,
Who give out thermal signals. Pure, demure,
They show, even when singing in a choir,
The lineaments of gratified desire.

Her parents were, for two nights, out of town.
When she and John wrenched their glued parts apart
No admonitory hagiographs gloomed down
Of Holy Family or Sacred Heart
Done in the Dublin style, thick-coated brown,
The piety more potent than the art.
Strict C. of E., she found it fun to doubt
God's seeing eye. Besides, the light was out.

Her father was a partner in a company
That specialised in oranges. They made
A decent profit, and they used to dump any
Gone putrid on to factories that paid
Not by the gross but by the sodden lump. Any
Orangy rot will do for orangeade
Or marmalade. They shipped them from the Bosporus.
The old man was illiterate but prosperous.

He did not much object to John Byrne's wooing
His little Sybil, and his literate spouse
Guessed what her giggling girl and he were doing
In the back parlour. Yet true love allows
Something more solid than mere billing, cooing,
Cuddling and kissing, petulance and rows.
But stern Victoria at this time was regnant,
And it was awkward when a girl grew pregnant.

Still, Sybil's mother's folk came from Glamorgan,
Where pregnancy was an engagement ring.
Accordingly she did not play the Gorgon
When Sybil blurted out that very thing.
The wedding would be now, with flowers and organ,
The bride in lying white, and John could sing
After, if not quite during, his own wedding.
Then there could be decorum in their bedding.

The father yielded to the nuptial knot
As fathers, pushed by mothers, always do.
John's dolled-up sister, best-man brother (hot
From stoking) looked, his snivelling mother too,
Uncomfortably alien in what
Was, in their native Irish papist view,
A church that God Almighty scowled upon.
This was no marriage. But it was to John.

It was, as well, a genuine advancement,
For Sybil's father fixed him with a place
Among the oranges. This citrous chance meant
Another insult to the Irish race,
According to John's brother, an enhancement
Of Williamite schismatical disgrace.
He'd wrongly smashed the fruit into a symbol;
His sense of history would fill a thimble.

So orange-fragrant John came home each day
To a mortgaged house, exiguous but clean,
Out of the noisy town, near Crosby way.
Sybil served up the Liverpool cuisine
– Lobscowse with oranges for afters, say.
He sang, she sang, they both sang; in between
They pedalled joyfully the nuptial cycle
And soon their son appeared: they called him Michael.

So Michael Byrne, the figurative bastard,
Entered the world smugly legitimate.
His father's seed had prematurely mastered
The conjugation of the verb 'beget',
But now forgot it. In that prim and plastered
Nest out at Crosby Michael was sole pet,
A kind of cuckoo-ego unsurprised
That later eggs should be unfertilised.

The Crosby bells clashed in this century
While Michael howled at cutting his first tooth.
A clash between his true biography
And what he swore was the untarnished truth
Is soon resolved. He loved mendacity
Especially when spelling out his youth.
And though his heart was all too glibly crossable,
Some of his tales are proved to be impossible.

For instance, he alleged that he was seated
Not far from Arnold Schoenberg on the day
That *Pierrot Lunaire*'s screams were first excreted;
He lent his fists to the ensuing fray,
Flooring a *Polizist*, was badly treated,
Then kicked out of Vienna right away.
A lad of thirteen? Such a lie is manic
(This was the year that ice struck the *Titanic*).

And then, upon the twenty-ninth of May
In the year following, he burst a fist
At the Théâtre des Champs-Elysées
When those who cheered were cracked by those who hissed
And vice versa. That well-known mêlée
Was in *Le Sacre*'s cause. Byrne would insist
That he'd kissed Diaghilev, also Nijinsky
And (the rhyme's unavoidable) Stravinsky.

Clearly a passion for the sonic art
Was something that his father's voice bequeathed.
Above the rhythm of his mother's heart
The foetus heard it long before it breathed.
Erotic soarings of a tenor part
Would soothe his gummy twinges when he teethed.
But he was destined to be less than awed
By songs like 'Come into the garden, Maud'.

In nineteen-twelve and -thirteen he was merely
Taking piano lessons at his school
(Protestant, secular – the terms are nearly
Synonymous). Though known as the school fool,
He won high-pissing contests and was dearly
Attached to heating up his somewhat cool
Female coevals with a slap and tickle;
He jerked his gherkin too, apt for a 'pickle'.

His father sang the tenor solo (badly)
In Elgar's famed *Dream of Gerontius*.
His son was there to listen, not too gladly,
Moved, though, against his will, by all the fuss
Of a huge orchestra careering madly
Through a next world weirdly euphonious.
He loved the tuba, trumpets and trombones,
Which smote his very scrotum with their groans.

He gained a chance to slide and lip and spit
Himself when, still a boy, he joined a band.
The war was on. He was not part of it,
Merely a junior munitions hand,
A teaboy really. John Byrne did his bit,
Serving the king of his adopted land,
Meaning he joined the Roosters, sang, wenched, boozed,
And oiled a rifle that he never used.

The trombone's a descendant of the sackbut:
Its music, solemn, martial, crisply clear, is
Produced by sliding forward and then back, but
You have to lip out the harmonic series
In something like an oscular attack, but,
In a young boy like Byrne, the action wearies.
An adjunct of the adult life is missing:
One needs the muscular panache of kissing.

The Industrial Revolution, Britain's pride,
Began, as we all know, in Lancashire.
It had a strong demotic cultural side:
Lest counter-revolution start to rear
Its snarling head, a salve was pre-applied
Whose safe cathartic properties we hear
In choirs that belt out oratorios,
And factory bands. Byrne played in one of those.

He played outside it too. At seventeen,
He put a Catholic Bootle girl in pod,
And, to avoid the inevitable scene
Of outraged parents crying out to God,
He swiftly packed a toothbrush and some clean
Shirts and, of course, the horn with sliding rod
(Both symbols of his sexual bravado)
And fled, like Nanki-Poo in *The Mikado*.

His mother, when she found him gone, was stunned.
There was a visit from a police inspector:
He'd taken nearly all the picnic fund
Entrusted to him by the band's director.
She howled, she was not far from moribund;
The news could hardly otherwise affect her.
His father came home with the armistice,
But neither got much pleasure out of this.

The gods of art were spitting on their palms,
So one might fancy, ready to create
A small creator who, unblessed by qualms
About the teachings of the Church and State,
Regarded prayers and penitential psalms
And all that truck as a sheer opiate.
Oscar had said art was above morality
Till the State buggered him for his rascality.

But national ethics, or what passed for it,
Had dumped some millions in the Flanders loam.
They whom the bombs banged or the bullets bit
(Trombonists were among them) had left home
For good, and some left places in the pit
Of the once famous Ardwick Hippodrome.
Here Byrne, though an apprentice still, got paid
To melodise, fart bass-parts, and glissade.

It was all conjurors and dancing dogs,
And veteran sawers of a girl in half,
Arthritic troupes that clumped about in clogs,
Comedians who never raised a laugh
Except in sentimental monologues:
Nobody ever sought their autograph.
But a soprano, once of the Carl Rosa,
Enabled Byrne to bud as a composer.

A faker really. Guinness on the brain
Had made this ageing warbler grow forgetful:
She'd left her music on the Sunday train.
The Hippodrome conductor was regretful,
But singers always gave the band a pain.
The pianist, asked to improvise, was fretful.
Byrne said he'd hammer band-parts out if she
Would name her songs and also name the key.

He named his price, of course. He knew about
The double-stops on fiddle and on'cello.
He'd read a book by Ebenezer Prout
And one by Higgs, both published by Novello,
And Stainer's *Harmony*. He had some doubt
About the pertinence of the old fellow,
Who said you could use that chord but not this chord.
The war had sanctified the use of discord.

17

He cobbled band-parts for 'The Holy City'
And Zionised the apocalyptic words
With little Jewish motifs, rather witty.
And for 'Down in the forest something stirred' 's
Banalities he introduced a pretty
Garland of rather Beethovenian birds.
The singer got the bird and he the blame:
She railed and roared but paid him just the same.

Public rebuke determined him to harden
An ego hard enough. He drank the cash.
The band played 'In a Monastery Garden'
And his trombone farted with dare and dash
The opening bars of 'Colonel Bogey'. 'Pardon,'
He belched, then passed out, falling with a crash
Into a drum, and drowned the solo flute.
That night he literally got the boot.

It was as well. His landlord's youngest daughter
Was two months late, she'd told him, with her menses.
The Bootle family was still breathing slaughter
(He wrote home, in abeyance of his senses,
Got that and, other, news). In short, he caught a
Vision of condign hell for his offences.
The thing to do when life seems all a-topple is
To run and hide oneself in the metropolis.

He played outside the London Underground
And found that coppers rather added up.
He paid his doss-house rent with a brown mound,
Ate saveloys, drank gin from a cracked cup,
And coughed a lot when wintertime came round.
The sad demeanour of a homeless pup
Along with a defective embouchure
Gave him, to lonely ladies, some allure.

A Lady Boxfox dragged him from the snow
And gave him welcome, warmth and wine and dinner,
The widow of an impresario
Who, when less prosperous and therefore thinner,
Patronised, without paying, Savile Row.
His suits exactly suited our young sinner,
Who showed his gratitude, or so he said,
By playing the trombone for her in bed.

There was a visit from a poor musician
Who taught in St Paul's School in Hammersmith.
His name was Holst. The German preposition
'Von' he had never been too happy with;
The war had forced him to its abolition.
Despite his Scandinavian kin and kith,
He was as English as Canute the king:
The English can make English anything.

Strange that the names of English-born composers
Should often sound (Delius, van Dieren) foreign:
Holst, Rubbra, Finzi, Elgar – names like those, as
Though the native stock skulked in a warren
Shivering at Calliope's bulldozers.
McCunn, true, rather overdid the sporran.
That Handel was staunch British to the end'll
Still be denied by Huns who call him Haendel.

Holst had composed *The Planets* some years back.
Byrne knew it, and he knew that the trombone
Had been Holst's instrument. There was a smack
Of fellow-feeling therefore in Byrne's own
Orchestral fantasy *The Zodiac* –
Twelve movements rising by a semitone
To come full circle. Byrne saw strange conflations
Between the key-ring and the constellations.

His lady took top-hatted Byrne to Goodwood.
Elgar was there, his sharp eyes on the course.
He couldn't help, but even if he could, would
It much avail? Music was a resource
Dumb to the English. Wait – Sir Henry Wood would
Air it perhaps. Look at that blasted horse,
Come nowhere, so much for the bloody favourite.
He groaned a groan but somehow seemed to savour it.

A baronetted masochist, thought Byrne,
Who'd slogged at art and fed his pearls to swine.
The English were determined not to learn
How to arrest their cultural decline.
Well, here's a David that will overturn
The assumptive glory of the Philistine.
Art, if it's pure, is hardly worth the candle.
They'll take it if it's seasoned well with scandal.

Wood, though reluctant, took *The Zodiac*,
And though the players found it fairly hard,
They tore it off with bulldoggish attack.
This was, of course, a summer Promenade.
The noise took the conservative aback,
But others cooed at it as avant-garde.
There are always intellectuals around
Who praise the incompetent as the profound.

Throughout the twenties, Byrne made little money
Out of an art deliberately dirtied
– *Absonderungstoffe* with a smear of honey.
His jazzed-up *Crucifixion* was asserted
To be foul blasphemy, and far from funny
Rabelais choruses that more than flirted
With the erotic and the lavatorial.
Would Mozart have liked this for his memorial?

Byrne found a theme in the *Decameron* –
The story of the devil put in hell –
And made a one-act opera. When put on,
In private though, it went down far from well.
The guests arrived, they gawped, and then were gone.
Not even postwar laxness could compel
Huxley, the Sitwells to find elevation
In naked howlers miming copulation.

And Lady Boxfox frowned her discontent.
She was not subsidising sweet sublimities;
Her protégé's pseudo-aesthetic bent
Was not for smooth silk or for flowered dimities.
She should have known the way his talent went
From his bed-prowess. Some men's sexual limit is
The pit. Its rage can find a counterpart
In how they mangle, tear, and rape their art.

And she was getting old, hence had suspicions
That Byrne clandestinely sought younger flesh.
For women, sense of smell, not intuition's,
The way to seek out perfidy, enmesh
The sinner in the guilt of his admissions.
She caught off bedward Byrne a whiff of fresh
Juice of arousal and cheap scented stuff.
The maid brought morning tea. She sniffed. Enough.

There was a screaming shouting snivelling trio,
With many a vigorous percussive burst
(Smashed vases, clanged Benares ware), a Cleo-
Patran storm alone for Byrne the curst,
Who cursed more loudly with Antonian brio.
He checked that he had pounds enough impursed,
Saleable silver. Baggage overflowing,
He slammed the door. He knew where he was going.

There were three sisters, not of Chekhov's breed,
Who lived in opulence off Berkeley Square,
All handsome girls, very well off indeed.
Their father, a dead Bradford millionaire,
Had left them everything but had decreed
The matrimonial act would strip them bare,
Ensuring that no idle wastrel would
Waste what he'd gained through sweat and bloody blood.

Bizarre condition! But they did not mind,
Since casual love sufficed. With Byrne's incursion
Into their household, they were pleased to find
One lover was enough, a rare perversion
Of patterns of the matriarchal kind.
Seraglios, whether Arab, Turk or Persian,
Are dreams of virile omnicompetence
Unratifiable by waking sense.

One of the sisters, Polly, painted prettily
And loved the ejaculative squelch of oil
In thick impasto that she'd learned in Italy.
Byrne left his hard compositorial toil
To wrestle with this craft, though rather grittily:
His vital function was, it seemed, to soil
(A twofold term implying health and tilth).
His paintings, in a double sense, were filth.

They chiefly showed the organs of coition,
Sometimes at rest, more frequently in action,
With hints of many a perverse position
Implying inadmissible infraction
Of copulatory laws. His exhibition,
Subvented by the girls, was an attraction
For amateurs of smut and not of painting.
The gallery was full of ladies fainting.

The London police, however, did not faint.
They clomped into the show in blue-clad torrents
And closed it down. In Parliament some quaint
Ruskinian terms expressed the State's abhorrence.
The same thing happened later to that saint
Of sexuality, the dying Lawrence.
Byrne felt the arrow of the martyrised.
He rather liked it, and he was surprised.

He did not like, though, in the local bars,
The nudge and leer of topers who suspected,
Except for more arcane particulars,
The nature of the life that he'd elected.
Aesthetic martyrs ought to kiss the stars,
Rejoice in being totally rejected,
And work away like disregarded beavers,
Unsubsidised by Harriet Shaw Weavers.

He left, but left behind a pregnant sister,
Granting to the triunal sisterhood
A task they realised should not be missed, a
Chance to do the maternal cause some good,
Anticipating later feminist a-
Ssertions that the male's sole function should
Be the provision of spermatozoa:
Show him that function, then show him the door.

The century had just passed thirty-one.
The Nazis, soon, would hog the floodlit stage.
But a more lasting movement had begun,
Possibly beneficial to the age.
Although the talking cinema has done
Great harm to the mimetic heritage,
In Chaplin's view, we must bow down to what
Progress decrees, whether we will or not.

Progress decreed Britain should join the rush
To fasten speech to faces on a screen.
The stories were a sentimental mush,
The ladies' accents genuine Roedean,
The gentlemen's a kind of thespian plush,
Unless a Cockney comicised the scene.
These British films were not well understood
By British ears attuned to Hollywood.

Byrne went to Elstree for an interview
And ended writing pseudo-music for
An Admiralty-subsidised *ragoût*
About the Navy's readiness for war,
With stiff-lipped skipper and a comic crew
Whose harmless booze- and punch-ups when ashore
Did not appear to lessen anyone's
Brisk readiness to rally to the guns.

With 'Rule Britannia' and the Sailor's Hornpipe
As *données*, all this frivolous sub-art meant
Sitting and dutifully grinding corn, pipe
In mouth and gin at hand in his apartment,
Often until the crack of queasy dawn (pipe
Of Tennysonian birds). And this new start meant
A new leaf, life, willingness to atone, a
Search for stability, a fresh persona.

He married Brenda Brown, who worked in make-up
– A cosmetician: God was not much more
(*Kosmetikos* from *kosmos*) – keen to take up
Domestic calm he once had thought a bore.
She was a decent girl who did not rake up
Harsh details of the life he'd lived before.
Happy in Morden, mortgaged, half-detached,
He fertilised her eggs. They duly hatched.

24

But during the long months of her gestation
He ground out music you can sometimes hear
In late-night films whose moral orientation
Speaks of a wholly alien biosphere –
Marriage without apparent copulation,
A Boy Scout code, social cohesion, mere
Euphemism, coiffured accents, desperate tedium,
Black versus white (appropriate to the medium).

Twins came while he wrote drone-stuff for some trash
About clan conflicts on the Scottish border,
A total failure, but it earned him cash.
And now three brothers with the surname Korda,
Who introduced Hungarian panache,
Preserved the industry from rank disorder
With quite a simple formula – i.e.
Make movies moviegoers want to see.

The Kordas were not insular – pelagic,
Thalassic rather in their visual vision.
They waved their Magyar wands, conjuring magic,
But were unwitting causes of perdition
To Michael Byrne. The technical term 'tragic'
Can be applied with absolute precision
When a man's inner but quiescent flaws
Are lashed alive by an external cause.

For Alexander Korda dreamed a drama
About the life of a tempetuous *diva* –
Tosca's *décolletage*, Brünnhilde's armour –
Whose voice attacked men's gonads like a cleaver,
The star to be a very *schöne Dame*
By name Maria Prauschnitz. She would weave a
Web to attract and finally enmesh
With diabolic pheromones of flesh.

25

She flew from Germany, gorgeous in furs
Against the fancied chill of late September.
There was one presence only – it was hers,
All fire, fire like the fifth night of November,
December Regent Street. As spring's scent stirs
The worm, she stirred the seed of every member
Of the small party Korda had convened
To meet her. Byrne reverted to the fiend.

She had survived abortions and miscarriages
As well as alcohol and drug excesses,
The ravages of four disastrous marriages
– Her fault – and yet with bright Teutonic tresses,
Teeth dog-clean, glorious body, there at Claridges
– The suite was one for shahs, sheikhs and princesses –
She shone, an icon of rich appetite,
A Nordic apple tempting men to bite.

But it was she who bit, bit till men bled.
She plucked, as from a male seraglio,
Byrne, to be borne unquestioning to bed,
There to be eaten with intensely slow
Rapacity till famine should be fed,
Then (*zum Befehl*) ordered to dress and go,
Discarded like a match or walnut shell,
The normal service of a good hotel.

She reckoned without Byrne. Byrne was a devil
Whose horns had been retracted for too long.
He bore her bodily to a deadly level
Where she was eaten, beaten like a gong,
Ox-roasted, in a blood-red reeking revel
Made to shriek sounds impossible to song
(He it was roared and crammed her opera house)
Except perhaps the *Salome* of Strauss.

She did not like the script that Korda proffered,
Scorned his associates as *Judenscheiss*,
Scoffed at the cash proposed to be uncoffered,
Naming a totally *unmöglich* price,
Wished to fly home on the next flight that offered,
Then, after alternating fire and ice,
With Korda in a most unwonted dither,
She limousined away. And Byrne was with her.

Aye, he is gone, seduced by his own glands
And a voluptuous Wagnerian vista.
Like the Commendatore's, see, her hand's
Immovably on his, a petrine fist, a
Faust. And he only partially understands
What life awaits beyond the German mist a
Speedy Lufthansa craft is butting into.
Think of the *Zukunft*? It would be a sin to.

Enshrouded, then, in a Teutonic mist
(*Mist* being dung in German), he's removed
From granting to a frank obituarist
The chance to list the actual and proved.
He's turned to matter for the fabulist,
A kind of Pan, hided, horned, haired and hooved,
Living with humanoids somewhat dissimilar,
Like Hitler, Goebbels, Goering, Hess and Himmler.

Maria Prauschnitz had a sumptuous dwelling
In Grünewald: it looked down on the lake.
Herr Rosenthal had needed little telling
To quit, rush the conveyance, also take
A sum absurd by the known rules of selling
And not to argue, for his comfort's sake.
The Nazis, at that time, did not abuse
The basic *Lebensrecht* of German Jews.

And, at that time, the swastika'd regime,
Compared with the Bolshevik cacotopia,
Had, to the world outside, a saner gleam,
Happier, healthier, even scented-soapier,
So Byrne's expatriation did not seem
A dubious one. The Führer's cornucopia
Of friendly undertakings, fruity, meaty,
Led to an Anglo-German Naval Treaty.

Yet Byrne could not forbear at times to wonder
Why State and Party should be unified:
The horseman in the saddle, the horse under
Were not a centaur. When he ceased to ride,
The horse would still be there. This was a blunder,
And when he made it conversation died
At gaudy parties where the Party boozed.
Joe Goebbels heard him and was not amused.

Shown Jewish blood beneath a microscope
And Aryan ditto on a neighbour slide,
Byrne said his mentors didn't have a hope
Of driving home a haemal Great Divide.
You had to drug yourself with Nazi dope
To see what seeing, damn it all, denied.
They're both the bloody same. The mentors hissed
And sent him to a Nazi oculist.

And Byrne refused to see how Jewish science
Could differ from the pure blue-eyed variety.
He argued: The enquirer puts reliance
On observation, not on racial piety.
Take Einstein, with his rational defiance
Of Newton and the whole damned Royal Society.
How the hell has his Jewishness impaired
The formula $E = Mc^2$?

Of course, his German was a sad affair,
Although he had an all too living lexis
In bed beside him, in beds everywhere.
But, as we know, the *Wörterbuch* of sex is
With absolute appropriateness stripped bare
Of such Hegelian wool as still perplexes
Students of philosophic German patter.
Gestapo cellars are a different matter.

Maria sang in *Carmen* and *Aïda*,
Die Meistersinger, *Tosca*, *La Bohème*,
And, to make merry her beloved Leader,
The Merry Widow. Everywhere her tame
Wild incubus the burning Byrne would feed her
Love (*love?*) unstained by shyness or by shame
And limitless in its varieties.
Her inexhaustibility matched his.

But he was much more than a sex machine.
His mistress, vamping Goebbels, soon secured him
The chance to write some music, crisp and clean,
To satisfy the guardians of the pure dim-
Witted doctrine of the foul obscene
Semitic threat. Mendelssohn, they assured him,
Dirtied Puck, Oberon and Bottom too
With all the black excretions of the Jew.

So, for the showing of *A Midsummer
Night's Dream*, Byrne wrote what was considered Aryan.
Carl Orff, who sniffed disdain at this newcomer,
Told Goebbels that the man was a barbarian
Who jointed notes like an unhandy plumber.
So he replaced him. In his unitarian
Heaven the happy Felix heard a lack
Of talent. Never mind. He'd soon be back.

Carl Orff's the sole survivor of the Nazis'
Conception of an Aryan aesthetic.
As soon as *Carmina Burana* starts, he's
Heard to be a phthisical diabetic;
Rich only in Teutonic grunts and farts, he's
Confounded the intoxicant and emetic.
And yet the ingenuous cherish every note
Instead of wishing that they'd cut his throat.

Byrne shrugged. He started writing a bravura
Opera based on Cleopatra's death,
Exploiting all Maria's *tessitura*,
With a high F before her final breath.
His hand had never, so he thought, been surer
In this her birthday (was it fortieth?
Fiftieth?) *Gift*, no, *Gabe* – was that right?
Yes. *Gift* meant poison, figuratively spite.

There was as yet no spite and little poison
In this, their sexo-musical ménage.
Byrne liked the German life, all brutal joys, an
Alpdrücken in a sensual camouflage.
Maria sometimes played with SS boys, an
Expected swelling of her entourage.
A goddess is, by nature, half a whore,
And Byrne required some semen for his score.

A heavy task, but there was light relief
In the Germanic ambience, boisterous, brash,
Torchlit parades and pogroms, guttural grief
In emigration queues, the smash and crash
Of pawnshop windows by insentient beef
In uniform, the gush of beer, the splash
Of schnapps, the joy of being drunk and Aryan,
Though Hitler was a teetotalitarian.

And Goering's weekends were a pagan riot,
With tough boar that his hunting parties shot.
Eviscerated stags reeked in a pie at
Which gormandisers gaped then scoffed the lot.
The Marshal's grossness publicised his diet,
But he was *künsterlich* as well. He'd got
Into his ringy paws a tawdry hoard
Of loot so vast the visitor grew bored.

Byrne was a foreigner, but it was felt
He was an adjunct to the Master Race.
His blood was right: he was a Saxo-Celt.
His voice proclaimed, an unambiguous bass,
The known resources just below his belt.
His German grammar was a foul disgrace,
But Byrne had his excusers and defenders:
Even the Führer could be weak on genders.

Moreover, England being called *Das Land
Ohne Musik*, Byrne was a kind of freak,
A singing starling or pink elephant,
An anglophone composer, quite unique.
Maria praised him as a *Musikant*,
Admitting, though, his counterpoint was weak.
Carl Orff assumed that Byrne would come a cropper, a
Jew who presumed to write a German opera.

Goebbels, in fact, had dug out the libretto
From dusty long-discarded juvenilia.
His cobwebbed attic was a kind of ghetto
To which, with an admitted necrophilia,
He stole to read, confirm and not regret. *O
Qualis artifex?* No. Too long familiar
With failed aesthetic power, he found it grander
To be the Minister of Propaganda.

31

His Führer's talent too was even littler
Than his. What if the aspiring architect
Had grown to be Herr Doktor Adolf Hitler,
An urbifactor, earning world respect
For soaring towers? No, nothing could be brittler
Than Adolf's dreams of what he would erect
– Sufficient for the whole Wehrmacht to enter –
Out there, the universal Civic Centre.

The poet as acknowledged legislator,
The trumpet also, singing men to battle,
Would soon shoot Shelley as a bloody traitor
And butcher other democrats like cattle.
The poet sees himself as a dictator,
But the dictator as a poet. That'll
Suffice, I think, for those who'd love to mix
Aesthetics with pragmatic politics.

The opus had its première in Berlin.
The Egyptian queen, a Jewish stereotype,
Seduced the Aryan Antony, and in
Her toils of grace, or her disgraceful gripe,
He sank into a slough of ethnic sin.
Maria was a wonder, rotten-ripe,
Capricious, sensual, serpentine or shrewish.
Her rivals swore that she was really Jewish.

The black-clad Roman chorus bore the swastika
On the triumphal banners they held high.
Antony perished by the traitor's law – stick a
Cyanide tablet in your mouth and die.
Egypt's destruction was near-holocaustic, a
Hint of what would be coming by and by.
The music pleased (it was not *nouvelle vague*)
Even the Führer, sparing time from Prague.

After this operatic consummation,
The already long liaison could not last.
Her enemies found sound documentation
Of Jewish ancestry. Agape, aghast,
She sought, in Himmler's high administration,
A uniformed protector, in whose past
Disreputable atoms lurked she knew about
But the hierarchy didn't have a clue about.

Byrne was alone, then, in a foreign city –
No, *he* was foreign, an exotic soul, and
Sat on the Ku-Damm with a cup of gritty
Cold coffee and an ersatz sausage roll and
Felt the authentic budding of self-pity.
That was the day Hitler invaded Poland.
He'd not been following the daily *Zeitung*.
He heard the news with wide eyes and a dry tongue.

A young man in the British Consulate
Informed him there was going to be a war
And he, though a long-term expatriate,
Could not expect to stay there any more.
Gather your goods and passport, do not wait,
Take train and ship to England. But what for?
Byrne wondered. 'England's rather more exotic
Than Germany, and – am I patriotic?

'No, I'm a son of Erin.' So he went
To Ireland's embassy to be assured
That strict neutrality was the intent
Of Ireland's government. Then he endured
A long wait for the Consulate's consent
To grant him a green passport. This secured,
He sat upon a bench inside the Zoo
And wondered what the hell he'd better do.

Now, from this point, like camels in the zoo,
We look upon a Byrne grown greyly distant.
He lived on Mühlenstrasse, Number 2,
But other vital facts soon grow resistant
To probings from embattled me and you.
Such talent as he had remained persistent
In wresting marks and pfennigs for a living.
History damns. Can we be more forgiving?

There was a Joyce (the ignorant said James)
Who quacked upon the Nazi radio,
Sneering at London going down in flames,
Spewing triumphalism, as we know.
'Regard,' said some, 'these two notorious names.'
(Mad Ezra's was the other.) 'Don't they show
That rampant modernism in the arts is
Soil for Fascisti, Falangists and Nazis?'

Now Byrne, the archives tell us, had the choice
Of spouting lies in his attractive brogue,
But he preferred a more impersonal voice,
Letting his flow of music disembogue
In major keys that seemed to cry, 'Rejoice.
Poland is crushed. And France. And soon that rogue
Elephant Britain and its Empire must
Tumble detusked and sobbing to the dust.'

The question is: Can music really speak?
Music is merely notes, all self-referring;
The articulative faculty is weak;
Music means rather less than a cat's purring.
The fact that E flat clarinets can squeak
Will hardly make them murine. So, in stirring
The listener's blood with crash and upper partial,
Is not a march a march, abstractly martial?

The situation grew more problematic
When German radio one night announced
A bass trombone concerto, acrobatic,
Scintillant, solemn. British listeners pounced
On Börn, composer, soloist. Emphatic
Newspaper leaders truculently trounced
Such treachery. 'We'll see the dastard swing.'
Meanwhile the BBC diffused *The Ring*.

There was no problem, no problem whatever
When Byrne or Börn took as a choral text
A passage from *Mein Kampf*. It was not clever,
Though some thought it ironic. It annexed
Motifs from Wagner in a coarse endeavour
To symbolise Teutonic muscles flexed
To kill the Jews, enslave the Slavs, and make
Six of the seas into a German lake.

His muse was silent after Stalingrad,
Save for some neutral children's *Weihnachtslieder*,
Settings of folksongs, neither good nor bad,
A funeral march for brass. The Allies freed a
Racked France whose anti-Dreyfusards had had
A hand in the *Letzte Lösung* but could plead a
Wretched enforced *devoir*, then crossed the Rhine.
Some looked for Byrne, but could not find the swine.

Byrne had, in fact, with little or no trouble,
Just taken refuge with the neutral Swiss –
Well, partly neutral. Always see a double
Aspect in disengagement such as this,
For even when the Ruhr was well-nigh rubble
Switzerland got its coal. The artifice
Of bleak indifference to the evil deed
Is justified by economic need.

And this explains, no doubt, the accommodation
The Swiss contrived with Nazi genocide.
The limit placed on Jewish immigration
Was, with a British Irishman, applied
When Joyce (for Joyce was Bloom) sought his salvation
In Zürich out of France fresh-occupied.
'The Jewish quota's full.' All Joyce could say
Was, so we're told, *'Enfin, c'est le bouquet'*.

Ethics and politics – ay, there's the rub.
Byrne, neutral Irish, could, as we have seen,
Live with the Nazis, in the very hub
Of infamy, morally not unclean
So long as he was silent. But the nub
Of his neutrality is seen to lean
On music's being dumb, hence undidactic –
A hypothetical defensive tactic.

Byrne got to Basle. A punished railroad system,
A purloined truck, abandoned, took him there.
A Germany in ruins hardly missed him,
So – *Sauve qui peut*. This was his own affair.
Though punitive invaders now would list him
A wanted man, Swiss bankers did not care.
He paid in gold in Zürich, quite a lot. It
Would have been rude to ask him where he'd got it.

We can see Byrne, smug with his Irish passport,
Sitting in cafés on the Bahnhofstrasse,
Puffing his Ormonds, sipping from his glass port,
Sherry, that gentian liqueur, seeing en masse a
Decent industrious race that could not grasp or t-
Est on the nerve-ends what had come to pass – a
Plunging of the real Europe into hell.
They'd had no history since William Tell.

No Alberich, though with his *Rheingold* banked,
He swived the insipid daughters of the Rhine
Or ladies of the lake, and then he cranked
The engine of a marital design.
He sought and found a *Witwe* – God be thanked,
Still young, Swissly attractive, on her vine
The grapes of what a billion-building zest
Had led to early cardiac arrest.

Reader, they married. After such collective
Villainy, what was bigamy to Byrne?
She did not trust him, but she scorned detective
Devices to dig up, unturn, and learn
The secrets of a soul perhaps defective
In Swiss morality. Still, Byrne would earn
His keep by, as the Swiss expression said,
Plying the fifth of five bare legs in bed.

A Northerner, she had the *Drang nach Süden*,
And so they set up house by Lake Lugano
To bask in Thyssen territory, Eden
With Adam Börn the snake, although there are no
Strong proofs of casual dalliance, indeed an
Impulse to sing *Là ci darem la mano*
To odd Zerlinas by Ticino's water
Only occurred when he had sired a daughter.

For, to give Byrne his due, he was a maker,
A natural father far more than a wencher.
Quite often the paternal urge will take a
Form that ignores the marital indenture.
Byrne was a bastardiser, not a rake, a
Creator, procreator. The adventure
Of art's not for the rubbered amorist.
Remember Byron, Balzac, Wagner, Liszt.

A minor artist with a two-stringed bow,
Byrne was encouraged by the southern light
To paint again, set up a studio,
Prime ample canvas and resume the fight
To show what no one really wished to know –
Sex, not in pornographic black and white,
But in bright hues – the rod's monstrosity,
The opposed pudenda and their rich pelosity.

Such paintings could not be exhibited,
For Trudi Börn spoke an emphatic *Nein*.
But one huge canvas, quite Guernican, did
Get private showing. Colour, contour, line
Crude but appropriate, it raised the lid
On the enactments of the Nazi swine,
Thickheadedness and thievery and thuggery
All symbolised in panoramic buggery.

After the *Corriere del Ticino*,
The *Corriere della Sera* ran
A brief report. Over her glass of vino,
Brenda, his true wife, visiting Milan,
Saw the name Michael Börn, brooded, could see no
Real reason why this should not be the man
Who'd left her nursing Timothy and Thomas
And forced her to a prosperous life of commerce.

By God, she would confront him at his villa,
Probably bigamist, certainly traitor
To her – to hell with country. Being no killer,
Merely a deadly cutthroat operator
In the cosmetic trade (name and sigilla
Would gain a certain fame a little later),
She'd merely break and bash, belt wounded cries out
And end by scratching (yes, by Christ) his eyes out.

And thus I would explain a gaping gap
In this, his brief but bestial biography.
He ran right off the European map
And learned a rather more outlandish geography.
He'd talent (recognisable) to tap,
But often changed his name with his topography.
Still, whether in Ashanti or Assam,
He's near-locatable: *Cherchez la femme*.

And, while you're at it, *cherchez l'art* also,
If you can call it that. For Byrneish trickles
Came out, with static, from the radio
In regions where mosquitoes bite, heat prickles,
Humidity is high and spirits low,
Concupiscence sporadically tickles,
And white men go to pieces, as we've seen
In overlauded trash by Graham Greene.

Byrne fled, it seems, in the late nineteen-fifties.
I visited Brazil in the mid-sixties
And in a Rio bar one day I sniffed his
Departed presence. For he had affixed his
Daubs to the wall in payment, no mere gift. His
Other bestowals toddled, for he'd mixed his
Blood with the octoroon proprietress's –
The swarthy blue-eyed fruits of his caresses.

I interviewed the Sultan of Brunei,
The richest magnate in the universe,
And heard that a Tuan Byrne had once been by
Running up debts and fighting drunk and, worse,
Smashing a certain *tungku* in the eye
And impregnating an *istana* nurse.
He left an anthem that was sometimes played
When the whole sultanate was on parade.

And in Chicago, in a low bordello,
I spied a dirty painting on the wall
Which mocked the sexual prowess of Saul Bellow
In detail which I don't care to recall,
A daub in mustard, chicken fat and Jell-O.
Libelling major artists, after all,
Portrays, betrays the doer, not the done to.
There was no calumny Byrne wouldn't run to.

This minor artist could be truly nasty
When sneering, leering at the real creators.
Knighthoods for services to pederasty
And CBEs to verbal masturbators
Were, naming names, among the slights he passed. He
Averred that earldoms only went to traitors.
A painted child of dirt, he stank and stung,
Daubing with digits dipped in his own dung.

You should by now be mildly interested
In me, who wear the obituarial robe.
Clearly no poet, all I ever did
In wordcraft was to prick and pry and probe
As an inferior pressman, salaried
To race for scandal round the spinning globe.
Byrne was good garbage for my garbage bin,
But usually got out when I got in.

Why choose this agony of versifying
Instead of tapping journalistic prose?
Call it a tribute to a craft that'd dying,
Call it a harmless hobby. Art, God knows,
Doesn't come into it. Poets, high flying,
Don't need these plodding feet with blistered toes,
Old-fashioned rhymes, prosodic artifice
Essential to an effect such as this.

Remember how I told you at the start
That Byrne himself commissioned me to fashion
A verse obituary. His own sub-art
Called for sub-art, not bardic skill and passion –
Base to the base, low low. A subdued heart
Beat with a carnal lust he'd learned to ration,
A late attempt to mortify the flesh.
I met him in a bar in Marrakesh.

What year was that? He didn't seem too old,
Tired rather. After a pink gin or three,
Fragmentarily, haltingly he told
Some of his tale. I wondered: why to me?
Two Berber lads with skins of tarnished gold
Came in. His sons. No, not sons. I could see
A change of sexual tropism. 'My boys.
I prefer women, but these make less noise.'

Where had he been? In India and Malaysia,
Contracting casual marriage. In Japan,
Like Pinkerton, he shacked up with a geisha,
After a Shinto ceremony, ran
Bangkok *kedùnkadìng*. All South-East Asia
Gained a lopsided view of Western Man
From Byrne, who relished his exotic cup
And wrote some music, though he tore it up.

Bull-charger, also silent-footed stepper,
Like Gauguin, he'd left paintings in Tahiti,
But not been made a syphilitic leper,
Placed his impress, all Celtic, boggy, peaty,
On girls' hibiscus, ginger and red pepper,
Quite unpolluted by a marriage treaty.
Marriage? A bed where two put twenty toes in.
Why should the church- or lawman stick his nose in?

41

I mentioned treason, but he merely shrugged,
Said something about signs, then dourly drank.
I didn't understand. The drunk, the drugged,
The overtly sodomistic sweated, stank.
The historic as the real – it beckoned, tugged,
Then shrugged like Byrne. Its fingers shrank and sank
Into the beer-slop. History is not tactual.
The factual is different from the actual.

Then 'Africa' he said. 'That's where we are,'
I said, sensing that was not what he meant.
He did not mean a mean Moroccan bar
Pitched on the bright edge of that continent.
A mirror of the Côte d'Azur was far
From what he meant. And far from where he went,
Yearning for mastication from the mouth
That chomped the jungle half-way to the south.

Chad, Mali, Côte d'Ivoire – where did he go?
A younger son bore documented proof
That Byrne had sired him in the place we know
As Happy Valley, under a red roof
Of Kenya. In his accent there would glow
Aristocratic gilt – a lilt, aloof,
Learned from his mother, who had walked with kings
But died of drink and drugs and other things.

One truth we know: two artefacts emerged
Ex Africa. Buffalo hides were sewn
To mock a canvas, and some impulse urged
The manic Byrne, with feathers, hairs and bone
And stone-ground paints, to craft a scene that surged
Junglelike, tenebrose, screeching. It was shown
In Cape Town but was soon incinerated.
It stated what had better not be stated.

The other work was musical, a setting
Of passages he'd taken from *The Heart
Of Darkness*, Mistah Kurtz's death begetting
A nightmare vision very far from art,
Since sounds should not be bistouris for letting
Black blood and ripping bones and veins apart.
Brian, his son, said that the opus swarmed
With screams and howls and could not be performed.

I leave his story here. *Assez. Es ist
Genug. Basta*. I think that Byrne is dead.
None left alive are going to insist
On heaping obloquy upon his head
– Failed artist but successful bigamist,
Thief, fornicator, traitor. I have said
Enough. I'll need a little time to find
Details of those poor sods he left behind.

Why did I do this? Further subsidies
Never arrived, but cash was not my aim.
A bastard, in no metaphor (that's his
Chief attribute), I spoke my mother's name.
He leered and said, 'My own paternity's
A possibility. I'll take the blame.
Be generous in your turn, do what I ask.
Think of a filial not venal task.'

The fascination of the reprehensible
Is my true driving force – was, I should say.
There's no defending of the indefensible,
No armature to strengthen feet of clay.
Wretches like Byrne are far from indispensable,
A single puff will blow their dust away.
Paronomasia is a needless joke:
He needs no fire to turn him into smoke.

TWO

I'm bedded down, it seems, in this hard stanza;
I cannot rise and rinse myself in prose.
Once, in an army cookhouse, with the pans a-
Wash in spuds I'd peeled, the thought arose
That I was a mere adjunct. (See, that man's a
Spud-peeling fist, no more.) So I suppose
I'm now an iron pen penning the ironical
Filial sequel: Father Byrne, his chronicle.

The technique should be much more novelistic,
Occasionally even microscopic,
Hairs and moles noted, if my masochistic
Adherence to this form allows – myopic
Close peering, and close listening to linguistic
Tropes in the thrall of an ephemeral topic –
What Booker fiction gives you every time,
Though never iron-corseted in rhyme.

My hero's a genetic violation
Of all his father stood for. He's a twin
Whose twin we'll meet some pages hence. His station,
The sacerdotal one, abhors all sin,
While Byrne the father made it his vocation.
He has small vices – cheap cigars and gin,
Whether of London, Cork, Bombay or Plymouth. He
Was christened, as you may remember, Timothy.

November thirtieth, feast of St Andrew.
He limped from Green Park tube. The air was tepid.
Unseasonable warmth possessed the land. Rheu-
Matically wincing but intrepid
He made for Curzon Street. His bare right hand drew
A hanky out, to wipe. Westward, a lepid-
Opterous sky, filigree, polychrome,
Called secretaries, sparrows, salesmen home.

The icecaps were fast melting, were they not?
The poles were yellowed with a filthy shroud.
Dirty the London sunset too, but what
Sumptuousness. The sackbuts cried aloud
In pageant, gaudy fabrics all aspot
With grease insoluble. An age endowed
With the dry cleaner's blessing made mad sport
With a crepuscular mock-Tudor court.

His left foot winced. The hallux nail, ill-cut,
Assailed the neighbour toe with a shrewd nip.
Did that toe have a name? He thought not, but
Knew his nine fingers had. Five gripped his grip
(Sensible term, American). His gut
Tensed as he passed a glottal fellowship
Of earringed louts shaved bald, swastika-belted.
Ice stood for order. Order too had melted.

He was not yet one of the feeble old
On whom bagsnatchers preyed. But, fifty-five,
Five feet six inches short, greyish, rolled-gold-
Framed-spectacled, an inner self alive
Enough, the fleshly shell though dull and cold
Without the ictus needed to survive.
Even if he'd dressed clerical, not laic,
He knew dog collars weren't apotropaic.

Whether that dress, vestments, collar reversed,
Was now to be legitimately his
He could not say – a thing to be rehearsed
In the long vigil of festivities
Named Advent, now beginning. If I'm cursed
Or blessed with death of faith, he thought, that is
A firm imperious signal that I must
Take better care of my decaying crust.

He reached his Mayfair target unmolested.
A hill of plastic bags proclaimed a strike.
His numb left foot disturbed a rat that nested
Inside a soup can. Someone's pedal bike
Distorted to surrealism rested
On old wet *Sun*s. With rictus of dislike,
Detaching shoe from shit, he danced it clean,
Then rang the bell of Number 17.

With his left thumb he pressed again that bell,
Born with no left ring finger, therefore slightly
Deformed, deficient. When his calling fell
Upon him like an enemy, quite rightly
The bishop had his doubts. He said: 'Well, well,
Nine fingers, nine, sufficient but unsightly.
Hands meant for handling the heavenly host
Should be equipped with ten of them at most.'

Priestly recruits, like those to the SS,
Should glow and grow in physical perfection.
Why, since perfection granted an excess
Of most unpriestly urges? The election
Of holy eunuchs should receive a yes
From the Lord God, who scorned the male erection
When, with his logos blueprint, he decreed
Insemination with no need for seed.

Dorothy came. He sketched the joky blessing
She much preferred to a half-brother's buccal
Kiss. The hall light-bulb had a most depressing
Low wattage. Mould and stalish honeysuckle –
The sempiternal smell. A more caressing
Odour – vanilla seemed somehow to truckle
To stern black chocolate she was always chewing
Through days and nights of ardent televiewing.

Her ragged crimson velvet viewing chair
Sat too close to the screen. That patient ray
Bit to the bone, they said. One of a pair
Whose twin held videocassettes – here TDK,
BASF, Fuji, Quasar, and there
Slept Sony, Maxell, Kodak. Briskly they
Were swiped by her to join those on the floor,
And on the mantelpiece were many more.

'Bibliomorphs,' he said, when seated. 'You
Need shelves and shelves and shelves and shelves.' But she:
'The cataloguing's slow, and labelling too.
Yukari helps.' 'Where is Yukari?' 'Tea,
She's making tea. You're late.' 'That's all too true,
The train was late. A long delay, you see,
Near Watford Junction. Their delay, not mine.
Something or somebody thrown on the line.'

Five of the eight bulbs of the electrolier
Were dead, one flickered. She seemed not to mind,
For all the light she ever needed here
Came from the TV screen, at present blind.
'And how is Manchester?' 'I rather fear
The Holy Name is going to be assigned
To mosquedom. The multiple muezzin's call
Reigns in a town where there's no rain at all.'

50

He peered at Dorothy in the dim light.
Celibate like himself, though for a lack
Of what was termed libido. Sixty. Sight
Focused on worlds within. Hair dyed bold black.
A demure dinner dress that once was bright
Near-orange, frills of dirty lace. A slack
Sack bosom, ample though, from which depended
Smeared spectacles whose legs had been ill-mended.

Rattling approached. Yukari, dressed in shorts
And FUCK YOU T-shirt, bore a kind of tray
Equipped with two unfolding short supports.
Tim felt relief: tea in the British way,
A big brown pot, a milk jug, cakes of sorts —
Ricecakes. She munched a raw fish canapé.
'Ikaga des' ka?' Western-eyed, she eyed
And munched and 'Always very good' replied.

A jasmine odour reeked from the weak tea.
Dorothy took one sip, then a cassette.
'This came as a surprise, this you must see,
Hear rather,' and with ghastly deftness let
A boisterous teenage nonsense scream its glee,
Soon quelled. Then static danced a minuet.
A cinematic logogram came on:
Eros-Film, with a firing cupidon.

When Foes Are Friends. This was the spotty title,
The music nautical and shrill and rough.
The credits came, a names-unknown recital
With Michael Byrne, composer. 'That's enough.
A tolerant world. A posthumous requital,'
He said. She said: 'It's early morning stuff,
Meant, I suppose, for empty-headed laughter.
Harmless. It's not the harmless that I'm after.

'I want iniquity.' Tim said: 'I know.'
'Law fish?' 'You know I hate it.' 'Nagasaki.
You there once.' 'Nagasaki. Even so,
I hate it.' 'Hiroshima too. The black i-
Niquity,' said Dorothy. 'A foul show
Of sin. The boot in. Racial hatred. Paki-
Bashing is in the dictionary. Rape
And torture. The whole world's in rotten shape.'

'More tea?' Yukari offered. 'Pardon me,
Deeply regret, and do not mean offence,
But as to tea not much strength.' 'Ah. Strong tea
Not good thing. Like that thing. You got no sense.'
Stink of his cheap cigar assailed. And he,
Inhaling deeply, said: 'You're right, and hence-
Forth I must watch my body, must I not?'
She nodded, chewing. 'Only one you got.'

'Are you still going to your English classes?'
'Big time waste. Evening work at Mr Wu,
It Chinese restaurant. Serve drink, wash glasses.
Is run by Japanese.' Probably true,
The time waste. 'I go light the boiler gas. Is
Bath time.' She left with table. How she drew
Him back – the Nippon mission, flowering cherry, money
Scant, a much more leisurely tea ceremony.

Dorothy said, with sudden urgent fire,
'This is important. Proof of immortality.
Don't smoke.' He went on smoking. 'You require
Reverence. I see.' 'I'm reporting actuality.
Joan Etheridge. Her heart stopped. Someone by her
Recalled her to the state they call reality.
Dead for the one split second, but was hurled
Into the world I call the real world.'

'Do tell me more. But not much more,' inhaling.
'She said,' she said, 'it wasn't like a dream.
A great grey hall, a counter with a railing,
Giggling girls. And there was a long stream
Of people moving, a loud hailer hailing.
You joined one team or else another team.
A screaming infant had to leave its mother.
It went in by one door and she another.'

'Just the two doors? No purgatory, limbo?
'Don't scoff. They beckoned her, but then she came
Back to this world.' Dorothy, arms akimbo,
Stood glowering. 'What do you want then — smoke and flame,
Angels with harps? *Maria e il suo bimbo?*
(They don't use that word right here. It's the name
They give the infant Jesus,' she said brittly.
'I ought to know. I spent a month in Italy.')

'Religion deals in faith,' he said, 'not proof.
And if my faith goes, this kind of banality — '
'That's the whole point,' she said. 'Rain through the roof.
Spit, rubbish. Bureaucrats' inhospitality,
Fag-ends on which some oaf had stamped his hoof,
A summing up of daily factuality.
Then immortality.' 'I'm tired,' he said.
'Wrap up your rhymes. I'll lie down on the bed.'

'Wait,' she said sternly. 'Have you made your mind up?'
'I have the whole of Advent to decide in,
But my last sermon was a sort of wind-up.
The Ultimate we usually divide in-
To the eternal three. But we may find we're lined up
To face eternal nothingness to hide in.
So we must worship zero — faith, no hope.
That negativity won't please the Pope.

'I'll live by begging you for the odd hand-out.
I won't. I'm joking. You need every cent
For videocassettes. I have a plan (doubt
Occluded, faith a lie) to pay the rent:
Working on holy TV scripts. Demand out-
Weighs supply, I think. That series went
Down rather well. It had a Spanish backer.
St Francis Xavier's thumbscrews in Malacca.

'I look to Robert Southwell for my bread.'
'Him I don't think I know.' 'I'm not surprised,
There's no cassette about him. Southwell bled
And screamed from frightful instruments devised
For Tudor Jesuits. When almost dead
From hanging, with his balls and guts excised,
He saw his heart. I rather feel for him.
He grants an aromatic pseudonym.

'He was a poet too. Perhaps you know
"The Burning Babe".' 'Horrors are no new thing.'
'This was a holy metaphor, to show
Christ as an infant but incendiary king.
Anyway, Robert Southwell has to go
Tomorrow for some gentle bargaining
With two Americans, who'll hear my line
On a filmed life of Calvin, the foul swine.

'What they propose could, I suppose, come under
The heading of a moral entertainment,
Like what, thanks to this electronic wonder,
You try to justify the world's arraignment
At Nobodaddy's court with – daily plunder
Of sempiternal horrors. Human pain meant
But little in the Gulf War's visual grammar, a
Big feast of death to feed the cinecamera.'

She said: 'It's horror, horror all around.
Pornography, locked in this cupboard here.
I wouldn't want that garbage to be found
By young Yukari.' He said: 'Have no fear.
The nerves of Nippon are all overwound
With overwork. Pornography's a mere
Device to them to get their nerves unlocked.
Yukari, I assure you, won't be shocked.'

'The point is this,' she finally confided.
'There has to be eternal chastisement.
That means eternal life.' 'A bit one-sided,
All stick, no sugar. Listen, we're all sent
To one big bedroom, Hitler undivided
From John the Twenty-Third, the innocent
And guilty, raped and rapist, with no cup
Of tea or orange juice to wake us up.'

He climbed the stairs to rest. Her television,
At rest too long, excreted into rock
That sounded like a motorway collision,
And then some politician's poppycock
And counter-cock pop-popping with derision.
They had to leave the house at seven o'clock
To see a show composed by their half-brother
And then to hear from him something or other.

Two frames were on the landing: Bradford bully
Bloody well bursting with his bloody brass;
Then the three daughters, features somewhat woolly,
Gazing with awe at daisies in a glass,
Painted by Polly, who had far from fully
Mistressed the killing craft, but let that pass:
A dull memorial to three unmade maids
Blown up in Florence by the Red Brigades.

Dorothy saw them as a triune mother.
They'd been unable to legitimise her,
But their joint legacy was a sort of smother
Of hungry love. She should have had a wiser
Load of investments, for some voice or other
From the next world had tried to pauperise her.
Still, though debarred from jewels, Jags and jets,
She'd not need to recycle her cassettes.

He found his room. The linen was unchanged
From his last visit, fifteen months ago.
There was that dried emission. One thing strange d-
Eclared her new obsession: a brief row
Of video recordings was arranged,
A kind of breakfast menu, as to show
A choice of Afghan rapes and Kurdish sorrow
To guarantee dyspepsia tomorrow.

He doffed his shirt and took his shaving gear
Into the bathroom. Steam. Yukari, clean,
Soon to be cleaner, lay in the water. 'Here.'
Western-eyed, illubricious. 'What this mean?'
He wore no spectacles and had to peer
Into the blaring porno magazine.
She read and frowned, raising a little ripple.
He had to bring his sight to her right nipple.

'It says that man is being pedicated.
The picture shows it, no need for a text.
You understand?' Unshaky hands gyrated
The razor handle, fixed a new blade; next
He aerosoled his cheeks with cream and grated
His tough beard off, embarrassed, somewhat vexed.
A priest should be impervious to shocks:
A bathtub was a wet confession box.

The Japanese saw aqueous immersion
As purely social, with all sex expunged.
Still, as the girl dripped out, a strong incursion
Of male resentment grew erect and lunged,
Her pedicable arse a wagged assertion
That he was neuter furniture. He plunged
Nine fingers in to splash his face and swore.
'True, I'm a priest, but also less, or more.'

Yield to response, pursue her dripping bareness?
Would she object? But that neat body seemed
Forbidden territory. Vague awareness
Of something in those Western eyes unsteamed
His lustful own. So like his own. In fairness
He must discount that, since the whole world gleamed,
Was hirsute with, was odorous of fair women,
A beckoning bare bath for him to swim in.

Yet, on the concourse of Grand Central Station,
You could meet someone met in Hyderabad
Twenty years back. Promiscuous copulation
Sowed perilous seeds. True, he had always had
A sense, by virtue of his ordination,
That women were his daughters, sisters. Mad
Semantics. Think: Greek incest had been banned,
They argued, to let family land expand.

Yukari had responded to an ad
Of Dorothy's, two years ago: 'Assistant,
Light duties, evenings free.' She said she had
A Western father, fled to somewhere distant.
Student of English, yes, but very glad
To stop, too dull. Probably unresistant
To proffered mistressships, but tired of these:
Why come to London to please Japanese?

57

Japan had won the war. The rising yen
Shone like an alien sun in sunless England,
With surplus yen exporters, bowing men
In hotel suites, condemned to travel single and
Happy to contact native flesh again.
There is a point where cultures will not mingle and
Bare bodies built on beer, beef, chops and cheese
Nip the concupiscence of Nipponese.

He smeared some aftershave called *Mansex* on,
Nudging his way into the secular scene.
Her high heels clacked, a door slammed. She had gone
Off to help serve the Cantonese cuisine
As rendered by the Empire of Nippon.
Still, the same ideograms spelt out Chow Mein.
(He sat to clip his toenails, brown and brittle,
Dressed in his vest and pants, panting a little.)

He mused on history and responsibility.
Did it have some to us, or we to it?
Whose history? There was a crass futility
In the big abstract monster, composite
Of unrecorded lives, with glib facility
Moulded by swine like Hegel to make fit
Doctrines of an emergent superhuman
Ultimate shining but tyrannic numen.

History as race. His Irishry was myth,
Although his English mother used to rail
Especially when first confronted with
His statement that he'd found the Holy Grail
In Papistry. That Irish kin and kith
Had got at him, she'd rail and even wail.
'That,' he would say, 'dear mother, is half-witted:
No culture is genetically transmitted.'

His twin, at the same school, in the same form,
Had known no like flush of the soul's awaking,
A language boy. Her language had grown warm
When he learned German. They knew why. The braking
Of her vituperative engine, the stilled storm
Of prejudice had much to do with making
Her products' name in Europe. Foreign commerce
Told her that they spoke foreign, just like Thomas.

He, Timothy, had studied at Maynooth,
Appalled at first – bog Irish ignorance,
And chauvinist perversions of God's truth.
He showed himself half-Irish in a sense,
Though hearing Irish phonemes as uncouth.
He modified his speech inheritance
(Pure Thames, or impure) to a diction fit
For a Britannic high-class Jesuit.

He now was nothing. Mother sometimes spoke
Of hating God, an allomorph of Byrne.
This ought to please her shade. Off with faith's yoke,
But she'd cast off all motherly concern,
Nursing her ailments among foreign folk,
Those of Antibes. Her flat, she let them learn,
Was on the rue Pasteur, where too a sort of
Catholic pen had scrawled, rather well thought of.

Really, he thought, he'd none to hurt or please. He
Was not betraying middle-aged parishioners
Who brought their secular sorrows, for the breezy
Brotherly Father Benlowe's cheery mission, as
Most had made clear, had rendered calm and easy
The shepherd–sheep relation. In addition, as
He'd dropped all doctrine, sin got not a mention,:
And God himself was trundled off, on pension.

History, then. He was not opting out of it.
He aimed to earn his living from demotic
Dramatic travesties thereof, no doubt of it.
St Stephen's martyrdom and crude erotic
Grapplings could share a soundtrack, just about. Of it,
The craft, he thought: I'll bow to a despotic
Technology indifferent to narrative,
Its visual values absolute, not comparative.

He put his shirt on. Carelessly he knotted
His only tie, one he had bought in Dublin
In '82, centennially allotted
To James Joyce junketings that caused some trouble in
Circles that said Joyce had defiled the unspotted
Image of Erin. Whorled Brancusi bubble in
A green pea soup, meant to be Joyce's soul
Or, not dissimilar, a cold ham roll.

He went downstairs, where Dorothy said, 'Look.'
He sat, he saw. The TV cameras panned
On Pakistanis and a burning book.
Not new news. Yes, it was. 'It must be banned,'
A Bradford Muslim leader yelled. He shook
An English Dante. 'Both the Prophet and
His son-in-law have blasphemously been
Traduced. This is heretical and obscene.'

'But,' said the Chief Librarian of the city,
'Alighieri died in 1321.
No pressure brought upon our Watch Committee
Can force a mere sectarian writ to run.
He's an established classic. It's a pity
Mohammed is in hell, but what's been done
Can't be etcetera. Liberalise yourselves,
You Muslims. Dante stays upon our shelves.'

'Stay is the word,' said Timothy. 'And shelf,
If that.' Disquiet struck him, somewhat dim
But definite, for Thomas, not himself –
He wondered why. Dorothy poured for him,
Also for her, some Claymore, from a well-f-
Illed cupboard. Airport double malt. 'Here, Tim.'
'*Sláinte*. What do we drink to?' She was lost in
An instant's thought, and then she said: 'Jane Austen.'

She? Dorothy was totally without
Book-learning. Potted drama on TV?
Idealised unviolence? How about
Old Boney? Admiral Austen. War at sea.
The Grand Porte. Captive Christians shelling out,
Delaying forced conversion. Let it be
Indefinitely delayed. The hypocrite.
Christians and Muslims did not change a bit.

With blind skill she arranged a fresh recording,
(A red clock span, lights darted like a gecko)
Thus fixing, *in absentia*, some rewarding
Survey of dying rain forests, a dekko
At child abuse for afters. All this hoarding
Of pain (he drained his dram). Umberto Eco
Had artefact speaking to artefact,
Cold epilogues to follow man's last act.

'We go?' 'We go.' It was not hard to get
A taxicab in Mayfair. As they drove,
They saw, though Advent hadn't started yet,
A London glistening like a golden grove,
Even in streets where signs proclaimed TO LET,
The town all Danaë to coruscant Jove,
Excited crowds, like waiting for a war.
The driver merely ground his gears and swore.

Dorothy paid, and Timothy could see at a
Distance that her tip displeased the cabbie,
Entering first the coruscating theatre.
He saw a well-dressed crowd, while he was shabby,
Many, though not so many as there'd be at a
Smartish first night. Dorothy too looked drab. He
Was given stall seats, rather near the back,
Also a summons to a midnight snack.

Half-brother Brian's musicals were notorious.
He had four running now in the West End —
This; *Brother Judas*; the somewhat inglorious
Queen Thatcher; then a heterogeneous blend
Of Wagner, ragtime, raga, rage, dysphorious
Sex called *Wasteland* that did not quite offend
The Eliotians and amused the gallery.
It made some money for the widow Valerie.

Reading about the hell of Tom and Viv,
Tim half-believed that Brian could adapt
Even *The Critique of Pure Reason*: sieve
The tome into pure Kant, who, rapt, unwrapped
The Categorical Imperative
As medicine to a Europe tyrant-trapped.
The present opus was *The Time Machine*. It
Seemed to divert the thousands who had seen it.

The distant tinkling of a tiny bell
Somewhere along Tim's cortical corridor
Now tintinnabulantly tried to spell
A message, that, some sixty years before,
This project had been broached. He could not tell
By whom, but heard faint music. Brian's score
Erupted now and drowned it with its clamour.
Sitting, they yielded to generic glamour;

The glow of floats upon the silvered curtain,
Waved baton with a light upon its tip,
Orchestral glow-worm lamps, the briskly certain
Drum-thump, bass-bong, warm as a Gruyère dip,
A brass growl, saxophonic squirt and spurt, an
Insufficiency of strings, as always. Whip
Aside the tabs: *fin de siècle* décor:
A rather young Time Traveller takes the floor.

'Observe me trace,' he sings, 'this triple space,
With up and down and then across, and then
Across another way, but there's no place
To accommodate the simple question *When?*
If time's a true dimension we can pace
Or race or chase both up and down – again,
Again, again. Though you look dubious, I'm
Prepared to go off cycling through Time.'

Too many guests, too many servants, but
Structurally justified in a sung chorus,
Danced too, with skirts provocatively cut
Right to the thigh. 'Whatever lies before us,'
They chant and prance, 'must keep its door tight shut.
Whatever's past is past.' They sing some more as
The chronic argonaut (a protonym
Of Wells's own) mounts and the scene grows dim.

But, West-End-like, the engine coruscates,
And, by some trick of holograms, is seen
High overhead. A near-nude dance of dates,
Brilliant in darkness – 1617,
Then 1500, and so back, gyrates
To reach – harsh braking on the Time Machine –
To 1321, *anno felice*
For Dante, paradised with Beatrice.

63

But no felicity in this Middle Age
That howls aloud now with the injunction 'Die!'
Plague-stricken peasants limp about the stage,
Though stylised dance-leaps rather give the lie
To their professed debility. The rage
Of clerics, landlords, villeins, serfs rides high.
All fingers point in superstitious ire to
A lissom girl they've started setting fire to.

'A witch! A witch!' But 'No, I'm not!' she yells,
Her limbs and bosom glowing through rent stitches.
And then a bishop's tenor tone propels
The truth about all women being witches,
Save one. *Save one? Save all!* They clang the bells.
The fire, as voices reach their topmost pitch, is
Fast spreading, and she screams. The scene's obscene.
But then the god arrives on his machine.

Unpinioned, she is pillioned, and they ride
('The Devil, Devil!') to the Victorian era,
Or mean to. See the Middle Ages glide
Into the past – but no. 'Damn it. I fear a
Fault – a blown valve. It can be rectified.'
But still they hurtle back. 'What have we here? A
Gang of lolloping dinosaurs. I'll fire
My shotgun.' Bang. They gracelessly retire.

Then, with occasional humanoid intrusions,
He makes repairs and confidently sings
About an age of meliorist illusions,
Gas, electricity, and other things,
Science, an end to fideist confusions,
Socialists shawing upwards on webbed wings,
Mending old follies with a rational suture.
Apemen lurch on. She thinks this is the future.

On, on, into the real it. Notting Hill,
The girl consumed in a black bacchanalia.
'It ain't no sin,' black infant voices shrill,
'To roast them pigs with the pinko skin.' A failure
Of integration, says the Traveller. Kill
Or mutilate. I'll chew your balls, impale your
Prick. Recognition pricks, and he looks for
His house, replaced by a snuff porno store.

Two louts seize the machine, evaporate,
Then reappear, howling of horror, horror.
Police and the mobs now lock in mutual hate
(They saw a horror worse than this Gomorrah?).
Death dances off. The Traveller, isolate,
Wonders if he now dare fare forward for a
Glimpse of the final hell. Go back, you stranger as-
Tray. But Nietzsche said life must be dangerous.

Dangerous, dangerous. 'Were they right, I wonder,'
He sings. 'Stay as you are, refuse to move,
Brick yourself in, safe from the wind and thunder,
Stick yourself in a comfortable groove.
So, little dog, be safe and warm, lie under
A cretinous eiderdown. No, no, I'll prove
A man is not a dog. Dare the unknown,
Dismember Time and bite it to the bone.'

'A lot of nonsense.' Dorothy attacked
A small warm Gordon's in the theatre bar.
Most of the quack quack comments (quack) that quacked
Agreed. Tim said: 'I'm pretty sure there are
Remnants of Wells reserved to the last act,
Or so I heard. The sun a burnt-out star,
Dead earth, a pop song for its epitaph.
The end of man. Anything for a laugh.'

No Middle Ages now, with witches, warlocks,
Burnings and bishops. Pre-industrial man
(Smocked peasants who went aaargh and touched their fore-
                                                    locks)
Metamorphosed to the Victorian
Proleship that's now become the race of Morlocks;
Genetic mutants, each a Caliban,
Cannibal really, masticate *en masse*
The effete Eloi, once the ruling class.

The girl the Traveller lost in the first portion
Emerges as the blonde anaemic Weena,
Spouting unspeech, abetting an abortion
Of literate lyrics. Eloi croon and keen a
Crowing, Morlocks grind out a distortion
Of hound-howls, growls, grunts, while the Time Machine, a
Witness of hell, lastly at least can cough
Civilised language as it whistles off.

And so the end of time, the sun near spent,
A slowing earth, degenerate monsters. He
Lets stirring words crash through the firmament:
'Victorian man survives, Victorian me.
We'll conquer yet.' Drums and trombones give vent
To triumph, and the Traveller's home for tea,
Hymning an unborn flower in his lapel.
Curtain. The audience took it fairly well.

'Not enough songs. Otherwise not too bad.'
They filled a corner table in Bernini's –
Tim, Brian, Dorothy, the Cockney lad
Who took the lead, the girl who shared the scene, his
Bed-sharing girl in fact, a girl who'd had
Fire, fornication, and an esculent finis,
A sinuous, delectable but dumb thing,
And also the librettist, Norbert Something.

A *trattoria*, not a *ristorante*,
Full of framed portraits, spotty and cooked brown,
Of Gino's ancestors, all of them ante-
Rather than anti-Fascist: manic frown,
Lethal waspwaist, oiled quiff. A schoolroom Dante
Was in the hands of Gino, just brought down.
'I think it's Canto XXVIII,' Tim said.
It was. Gino melodiously read:

'*Com'io vidi un così non si pertugia,*
Rotto dal mento infin dove si trulla.
Tra le gambe pendevan le minugia – '
'Clearly,' Tim said, 'anathema to the mullah.'
'*Che merda fa di quel che si trangugia* – '
Tim slapped with an imaginary ruler:
'You've missed a line. *La corata pareva*
E 'l triste sacco. Don't dilute the flavour.'

'For ladies, no,' said Gino's fat grave grin.
'This lady didn't cop a dicky bird,'
The girl said, forking antipasto in.
'This is the content, though not word for word,'
Tim said. 'His body's split from arse to chin,
Guts hang between his legs, A wretched turd-
Outchurning sad sack, food to fecal stuff – '
Dorothy said: 'We're eating. That's enough.'

'Shit really, *merda*. Listen. "He gazed at me
And ripped his chest wide open. Thus I saw
Mohammed mutilate himself, who said: 'Now see
The weeping Ali – ' " ('That's his son-in-law')
" 'Face ripped from chin to hairline.' " He and he,
Sowers of discord, get their ever raw
Wounds rendered rawer: each demonic sword
Rams home the eternal justice of the Lord.'

'Where did you learn the wopspeak?' 'He's a priest,'
Brian unexplained. 'Dante,' Tim then expanded,
'I honour as a saint – well, blessed at least.'
The girl ate her *vitello* single-handed,
Munching: 'Do priests fuck now?' This priest released
Some rank cigar smoke with: 'Well, to be candid,
Some priests may snatch a fumble in a hallway
But leave the whole hog to His Grace of Galway.'

'Your thing was nonsense' (Dorothy). 'Oh, really?'
Yawned Brian, with the tone of Maynard Keynes.
'We thought we'd fixed a frame around it. Clearly
You missed that. I, with Norbert, was at pains
To flout progressivism and not merely
Construct a construct that – well – entertains.'
'Them big words.' The two Cockneys chewed like cows.
She spilt veal sauce upon her Magyar blouse.

Brian spilt nothing on T-shirt or jeans;
Even his Mickey Mouse watch appeared polished.
He did not flaunt blue blood by any means,
But no demotic stance could have abolished
The aristocratic aura. Kings and queens
Might see their ancient hierarchies demolished,
But he had been bequeathed a certain quiddity
Hard to define but of a hard solidity.

'I saw this TV thing – a second law
Of thermo something.' A duet: 'Dynamics.'
A solo: 'Entropy.' The girl's dropped jaw
Went 'Jesus.' Brian went on: 'Smashed ceramics,
Spilt milk, bombed cities all add one bit more
To universal breakdown's jar of jam. Ex-
Cept in films you can't wind back the action.
Addition's never fashioned from subtraction.'

'That's it,' Tim cried. 'A film that no one's seen.
When Wells had done his *Things to Come* with Korda,
He swore they'd follow with *The Time Machine*.
But "Music first, then script – that's the right order,
Like *Things*." But the composer Bliss had been
Disgusted by the soundtrack. "Can't afford a
Re-recording," Korda said. "Scraped tin,"
Yelled Bliss. And that's where you-know-who came in.

'Meaning there was a score.' 'There *is* a score,'
Frowned Brian. 'I cleaned up its bloody mess.
Later, later.' Their talk had been a bore
To one at least, who chewed: 'Do all priests dress
Like you do?' 'You mean scruffy?' She searched for
A word. 'Incog.' Norbert said: 'Mufti.' 'Yes,
Meaning an expert in Koranic law.
Afta's the root. My twin could tell you more.'

'You're seeing Tom?' asked Brian. 'Yes, D.V.
Venice, tomorrow.' 'Venice? Lucky you.'
'Not at this season, darling. Will you see
If Tom can knock us out a verse or two
In hundredth-century London English? We
Need something better for these two to do
Than amorous gibberish. It was bad tonight.
We're always mending aircraft in mid-flight.

'A musical is planned and replanned, rereplanned and
Planing and chiselling are never done,'
Gloomed Brian. 'On the last night it's abandoned.'
He signed the *conto*. Norbert: 'I must run.
Ta for the scoff. See you.' He waved his hand and
Left. To Tim the girl said: 'Bye, have fun.
Tutti frutti.' The Traveller, waving: 'Cheers.'
She: 'Give my love to all them gonorrhoeas.'

'Well, now –' Brian unleathered two Coronas.
'We have to talk about Byrne's resurrection.'
He lightered Tim's cigar and then his own as
Pangloss whispered to Tim of the perfection
Of God's creation, still but dimly known, as
The giant weed slid snug into the section
Undigited. God knew what he was at:
The nose for spectacles, and that for that.

The weeds, of course, had first been circumcised.
The golden cutter all the way from Tiffany
Brian now span. 'A concert I've devised,
And not for Easter but Polyphony,
I mean Epiphany. I realised
The scope when all that stuff came. Speak now, if any
Doubt's in your mind about the project's merit, as
You and your twin are the true sole inheritors.'

'Stuff?' 'Yes, his scores, sent to me from Nairobi,
Some paintings also. If I'm not mistaken,'
(Fingering the gold ring stuck in his left lobe) 'he
Was doubly great. We have to bloody waken
The bloody world to what it ought to know. Be
Ready for some shocks, though. Francis Bacon,
Now larded, lauded, being dead, knew terror,
But Byrne knew terror's mother, and no error.

'As for the music – well before its time.
Ironic sentiment. Inverted commas
Inside inverted commas. The sublime
Turned into slime. Street crime. The hum of bombers,
The crash of cities. Love. Reason and rhyme
Upon the rack. The bloody heart torn from us,
Messages, codes. And all that's just from grazing
The scores. The sound is going to be hair-raising.

'You, Dorothy, have those pictures at your place,
Daubs, you once said, that you'd be sick to see.
Let's have them out.' Disgust suffused her face.
'Cobwebs and filth. I threw away the key.
My mothers told me they were bestial, base
And brutish.' He: 'However that may be,
The properties belong to Tom and Tim.
Tim's here. Tom's there. It rests with him and him.'

Tim said: 'I can deliver Tom's consent.
You are the artist, sort of. So no no
From us layfolk. Posthumous punishment
Or pardon, which?' 'I only wish to show
Neglected talent. I've prepaid the rent –
The Barbican, also the LPO.'
She: 'Palestine? Tea-towelled Arafat?'
'The Philharmonic. You'll have heard of that.'

He puffed. 'Polyphiloprogenitive.
He wasn't negative. Is that a crime?
Is it a crime to live? He bade us live.
We are three bicycles that ride on time,
Forged in his gonads. And his works will give
Salutary palpitations. Therefore I'm
Firing his guns while he rests on in peace.
Nihil nisi nihil de mortuis.

'Shoving the needle in a different groove'll
Confound my bloody critics,' Brian said.
'Approval, yes? You're nodding your approval?
You're nodding anyway. It's time for bed.
And Gino here requires the prompt removal
Of bodies moderately drenched and fed.
Ci dispiace, Gino.' Out they got. A
Wide yawn caesura'd Gino's *buona notte.*

A Neapolitan – not just his accent,
Also a *cena* worse than mediocre.
Lacrima Christi's fumes, all lava-black, sent
A shaft through Tim hot as a sizzling poker,
While the half-smoked Corona answered back (scent
Of foul Cuban *retretes*). All bespoke a
Sore need in Tim to renovate his system.
He handshook Brian; his half-sister kissed him.

She bruised her lips on his designer stubble. 'You
Had best send Tom's approval in a fax.' 'He
Won't disapprove.' Then Brian's BMW,
Silver agleam, blue surface over-waxy,
Rolled up. 'You want a lift?' 'No, we won't trouble you.'
Less than imperiously Tim hailed a taxi.
The chauffeur opened up, Brian was sped
Home to his catamites and triple bed.

'Recalled to life,' said Dorothy. She'd seen
That Dickens thing in 1989,
When, to mixed feelings, *la Terreur* had been
Unbottled like a long sequestered wine,
Reminding Europe what *l'Europe* could mean
If France's ideologues kept it in line.
'Recalled to life,' twice or thrice more she said,
Like Dickens, adding: 'Is he really dead?'

'As a doornail.' Tim cited the same writer.
'Definite from the Lagos legation.'
He read NO SMOKING, put away his lighter,
And said: 'Call Brian's thing the last purgation.
Let the old bastard take a final bite, a
Bold nip at ears and eyes, be a sensation,
And then, insensate, yield to the worms' hunger,
Deader than what you get at the ironmonger.'

She opened up and hurried in to check
That her indifferent video recorder
Had chronicled Brazil's arboreal wreck
And, here at home, domestic sin and sordor.
Timothy eased Brancusi from his neck
As she called up: 'Everything is in order,'
Like a returning housewife glad to learn
The puppy didn't shit or the roast burn.

He woke at three, nursing a half-subdued
Engorgement helped on by the tears of Christ.
Unchain the beast after long hebetude?
Odd heavy-breasted images enticed.
He thought he heard tiptoeing feet light-shoed,
Yukari's whisper. Flesh that was too long iced
Must melt, the Time Machine be oiled. Inept
Prospective rider. Jesus wept. He slept.

Yukari, bright at eight, brewed him strong tea,
Squeezed orange juice, cooked British sausages.
'*Choozume*.' Tim wondered why that should be,
Origin Spanish. All these mysteries.
'No, no, this sausage. Different thing.' And she
Among the old copper solidities
Showed herself a true daughter of the sun
With microwaves, sung signals of toast done.

'In Nagasaki you eat sausage?' 'Canned.
Our brotherhood was British and frustrated.'
Frustrated? A slight tremor of the hand.
Yukari's very British apron dated
From when the Union Jack had been a brand
Of hedonism jokingly related
To patriotism, the beginning of
Sexual intercourse, though hardly love.

Beneath she wore knickers and brassière
Of chocolate-coloured substance. He had read
That one could buy esculent underwear
And wondered was this it, but ate instead
His sausages, baptising the brown pair
With IQ sauce. He, crunching toast, then said:
'Were many there at Mr Woo's or Foo's?'
She also wore, he noted, high-heeled shoes.

'Good tip I get. Here she not pay too much.
More good she not. Not stay in all the night,
Watch *terebijon*. Here you not see such
Like Tokyo. More sexy.' Down the flight
Came Dorothy's fast feet. 'It I not touch.
She late for breakfast news. Not do it right,
She say, record wrong thing.' More sexy? Loud
Roared objurgations of a Muslim crowd.

Outraged believers in Islamabad
Demanded filthy Dante's execution
Outside the US Embassy. A sad
And academic voice poured a cold douche on
A hot *imam*. Iranian leaders had
As yet not issued a stern resolution
About the doing of the sinner in.
That would come with a later bulletin.

Dorothy entered in a dressing gown,
One of her mothers', doubtless, poured a cup
(The lacy nightdress too), said with a frown:
'How can you lap that horrid offal up
So early?' 'Priestly habit.' She sat down,
Tentatively taking in a scalding sup.
'Christ's body's insubstantial. Something ample
Must follow. John Polack sets an example.'

'Your staying here – will it be permanent?'
'Yes, if I permanently break the yoke.'
Mishearing (yolk) she retched. 'I'll pay you rent.'
She waved the rent away, with his rank smoke.
'Will there be women in your life?' The scent
Of dreams of armpits smote him as he spoke.
'I hadn't thought,' he lied. She weighed and gauged
And said: 'You're old.' He said: 'Try middle-aged.'

'He not.' Yukari seemed to ooze authority.
'Not fat. Some hair he got. And he got tooth.'
'Enough to bite your chocolate – Sorry, sorry.' Tea
Gulped washed down his embarrassment. Uncouth.
He'd never spoken thus to a sorority
Of virgin fillies, doling out God's truth.
Yukari pinched his flesh, as of a Christmas
Turkey. She had a sweet morning strabismus.

'I get that thing.' 'What thing?' 'To make hair black.'
She raced off with a flash of bold bare thighs.
'You need a suit,' said Dorothy. 'You lack
The look of one who's used to high-class lies.'
Shrewd, very shrewd. He said: 'I'm bringing back
Old clothes Tom doesn't need. We're size for size.
Even perhaps some clobber apt for tennis.
Tom said he'd bring a suitcaseful to Venice.'

'Is Tom in pain?' 'It's eased with Tetraphone
Or Trampoline or something. The cold steel
He naturally wishes to postpone.'
'God, where's God's justice? Don't you ever feel
It should be you? On TV twice they've shown
This Early Church thing. They said holy zeal
Made this man do it with a single snip, as
Easy as cutting nails with your nail-clippers.'

'Enervate Origen.' 'I didn't catch
His name.' Yukari dashed in to deploy
A brush and bottle on his thinning thatch.
He read the ideogram which said *kuroi*,
Or black. She blacked his eyebrows too to match.
Curious: an image of a Polish boy
As she removed his glasses. His libido
Seemed to await redemption on the Lido.

Dorothy too caught swiftly the similitude:
She knew at least Visconti's masterwork.
'This will not make you change your nature, will it? You'd
Better not turn into a sort of Dirk
Bogarde. Disgusting. And the silly billy chewed
Infected strawberries. Some folk go berserk
In Italy, especially old men.
It's AIDS now, but it was the Black Death then.'

Yukari womanhandled him to show
Tim Aschenbach, moustacheless, in the glass
That flanked the cooker. So, then. Time to go.
He kissed her porcelain cheek, patted her arse,
And gave her *'Kansha suru'*, bowing low.
For Dorothy he made a priestly pass,
Gripping his grip. 'My love to Tom, remember.'
'God bless.' He strode out into spring December.

Green Park to Piccadilly. Bakerloo:
He rode to Oxford Circus, Regent's Park,
And last to Baker Street. A twinge or two,
Rheumatic. Glassless vision blurred the stark
Outlines of things. A gritty warm wind blew
Spent fastfood cartons. Foreign races, dark
And not so, milled possessively about.
The Anglo-Saxon breed was dying out.

Ten five. A little late. He had to hurry
To Dorset House and Brian's agent's office.
The ground-floor Crown of India breathed faint curry.
The porters, ebonite and milky-coffee-s-
Kinned, sent him up. He tasted a slight worry,
For Brian's agent was a Shoreditch toff, ess-
Ential barrow boy, East Endly fecular,
Totally absolutely crassly secular.

He was already slitting open mail,
Dressed as if to engage the Stock Exchange,
One of the money bugs poised to prevail,
Agential boasting in a four-walled range
Of naked posters whose wide spectrum – pale
To puce – would irretrievably estrange
The Calvinists. 'No problem. Go in there.
We wouldn't want to give the sods a scare.

'The pen-name's Southwell, right?' That pseudonym
Grew shady here. *As I in hoary winter*
Night er stood shivering – ' Tim gaped at him
In disbelief. 'Er *in the snow –* ' A splinter
Of culture? 'Er *Surprised I was –* ' The dim
Glow of a soul? '*By sudden heat –* ' A hint, a
Wink of heaven? '*That made my heart to glow*.
That wouldn't make the top ten, would it?' 'No.'

'But always do your homework, sunshine. And
Always have coffee ready for the Yanks.'
He set it bubbling with a practised hand.
'You want some?' 'Makes my heart to thump. No, thanks.'
'Don't mention fucking money, understand?
These fuckers have no problems with the banks.
They own the fucking things. Calvin was Swiss.
We'll make a fucking killing out of this.

'They're 'ere.' They were – the Reverend Eli Sewall,
Sam Wadsworth. Tim asked the grim cleric whether
He was of the diarist Sewall's clan. He knew all
Of one brief entry: *'Swallows, six, together
Flying and chittering rapturously.'* 'You al-
Ready got 'em?' – Wadsworth. 'Crazy weather.'
'No, I cite Sewall. "Chittering" is superb.
Chitter – a good old Massachusetts verb.'

'No time for chitter, chatter. We admired
Your film of the Malacca colony
And how those lax Mohammedans acquired
A less lax Catholic Christianity.'
The Reverend beetled. 'But was it inspired
By your own – ?' 'Never, sir. My sympathy
Is all with faith expressed in rigorous laws,
Commitment to the Calvinistic cause.

'My life, you might say, has been dominated
By an innate Genevan point of view.
British permissiveness has nauseated
A soul essentially ascetic. True,
I've Jacob-wrestled with and execrated
Slimy seductive devils of the new
And won, I think. Now I can laugh at Rome
And Canterbury too. I'm safely home.'

'You've been in orders?' – Sewall, rather shrewd.
'My talent's propagandist, hardly pastoral.
I've brooded and pursued in solitude
A methodology to make our Master al-
Ive, a living force. However crude,
A film that screams of imminent disaster, al-
erting us to God's, or Calvin's, wrath,
Is solid meat. Sermons are tepid broth.'

'*My* broth was well digested in its day,'
Said grumpy Sewall, every inch the cleric. A
Savile Row suit showed Wadsworth to be lay.
(His cupric hair opposed his partner's ferric.) A
Card he now proffered said: 'CLNA:
The Calvinistic League of North America.'
'That's who we are,' he said. 'And now you know –
The offspring of the *Institutio.*

'John Calvin's life – twelve one-hour episodes.
That's what we want. Think you can undertake it?'
'I sure can,' answered Tim. The breezy modes
Of US speech came naturally. 'Make it
Convince, hit home, impress, cram it with loads
Of flesh and blood. For sweet religion's sake it
Has to have impact, right?' He added: 'Wham.
Ready to go?' Timothy: 'I sure am.'

'The Calvinistic epic must be told,
Resistance to its message overcome,'
Said Sewall, 'seen and heard, above all, *sold*,
Bringing in an incalculable sum – '
(Here the back-seated agent slyly rolled
Mercurial finger against horny thumb.)
' – To finance missions in the name of Calvin.'
He seemed to suck a succulent bivalve in,

Though ready to regurgitate it whole
When Tim said 'Art'. Wattles somewhat ashake,
'Art,' he pronounced, 'misleads the human soul.
Art.' (Bitter capsule bitten by mistake.)
'It devastates all spiritual control.
Pernicious doctrine – Art' (gulp) 'for art's sake.
It led your Oscar Wilde to condign hell.
We want no art. We want the thing done well.'

'OK, let no seductive art intrude,' ass-
Ented Timothy, adding 'He's not my
Oscar, by the way. There'll be no crude ass-
Ertions of the flesh.' 'We want this guy,
British of course, that I saw playing Judas.'
Agential interest but a sort of sigh
From Sewall. A sign-of-the-cross nostalgia?
The sort of wince that's ground out of neuralgia?

'A transatlantic voice would be inept,
I take it?' 'Calvin was a European,'
Said Sewall gravely. 'French.' Regret had crept
Into his tone. 'But soon we hope we'll see an
Epic account of how New England kept
The faith, a supreme televisual paean
To what became American theocracy,
Vox populi vox Dei, hence democracy.'

Timothy offered: 'The late Van Wyck Brooks
Regretted there's a truth you'll hardly find
Registered in the US history books
About the making of the US mind –
It's Janus-faced, with contradictory looks:
Two equally unsocial trends, a kind
Of transcendentalism, idealistic,
And the catchpenny –' *'What?'* – 'Opportunistic.'

The listening agent, hearing hints of cash,
Made a throatcutting gesture, frowning much.
'A European?' 'No, a sourish mash
Of Pilgrim Father and commercial Dutch.'
'Wholesome mercantilism libelled by a brash
Uncalvinistic sceptic.' 'Just a touch.'
'You've read quite widely.' 'Yes, even in odd
Corners of dusty libraries I seek God.'

'A question I must put – Michael Servetus –
What do I do about his martyrdom?'
'No martyrdom!' Sewall grew as irate as
If a crass hammerblow had smashed his thumb.
'Foul father of the Unitarian traitors,
He seethes in hell. Their hell is yet to come.
I shudder at that vicious analogue –
The Trinity as a three-headed dog.'

'I too, I too.' Sewall grew proprietorial:
Should they pay less for infranumerary fingers?
'Some accident?' 'Alas, the sad memorial
Of a quite unheroic act, a thing as
Common as dirt these days. No front-page story. Al-
Low me my reticence. The pathos lingers.
A little girl, a dog, the dog grew rough,
A Rottweiler. Its one head was enough.'

The contract? Contract. An agential nod.
'We pray.' Sewall flopped down with practised ease
Upon the broadloom, giving a sharp prod
To coffee-draining Wadsworth. Knelt. Tim's knees
Were calloused and habituated. 'God,'
Prayed Sewall, 'Look down kindly. If it please
You, let your servant tell the sacred story,
Nine fingers tapping your and Calvin's glory.'

He turned his black back on financial sordor,
Inviting Tim to lunch. Early and light.
A salad bar. Lettuce would be in order.
At two o'clock they had a Boston flight.
'Alas,' Tim said, 'or not. I too must board a
Plane, though Geneva-bound. Must get it right –
Predestination, banks and clocks, the sheer
Calvinity of the whole atmosphere.'

81

'Geneva.' Sewall swallowed somewhat sourly.
'The banks, true, are a Calvinist solidity.
Accurate public clocks remind you hourly
Of death approaching with its sly rapidity.
But sin and sex abound. There's lust's foul flower. Li-
Aisons, mistresses, *putains'* putridity.
The lewd proposal from the carmined mouth. Well,
Well, preserve your innocence, Mr Southwell.'

Innocent? He? The tube train to Heathrow
Threw up the debris of a tattered *Sun*.
His body did not lie, he gloomed to know,
Responding to its tits. What had he done
Mentally, morally? Glowed at the glow
Of thirty thousand dollars. He'd begun
The well-greased progress of the hypocrite.
Why, this is hell, nor am I out of it.

South Kensington, Earls Court, then Hammersmith,
Soon Acton Town, South Ealing, Boston Manor,
All stations of a shaky ligneous myth,
And *in hoc signo vinces* a torn banner?
Osterley, Hatton Cross. He got up with
His grip well gripped. His shaky limbs began a
Terminal search. Earth travel here hath ending.
He limped to his ascent, his soul descending.

Udara Indonesia first to Munich,
Then Alitalia for the other leg.
A beauty, half-Malay, in a tight tunic
Sold him raw gin, then served him a cold egg
On colder rice. He frowned away the runic
Of Oriental news sheets, had to beg
A dozing black's discarded *Telegraph*.
The news was good for a sardonic laugh.

But 'NOTICE: The failed artist Michael Byrne
Invites the fruits of his insemination,
Legitimate or not, to come and learn
His final will and testament. Location:
Claridges, London. Tourist air return
Fares reimbursed. Drinks and a cold collation.
At 8 p.m. this coming Christmas Eve.'
This was a thing that Tim could not believe.

But it was also in the day's *giornali*,
Seen on the Venice flight. Also *Die Zeit*.
Dead as a doornail? No, no Jacob Marley.
Le Monde. El Pais. Still alive, in spite
Of ninety-odd years' sinning. Fit to parley
With truculent descendants on the night
When shepherds glimpsed an untoward stellation
And Scrooge was smacked to his regeneration.

Tom too had seen it. Tom awaited him
At Venice airport. Rain smacked the lagoon.
The empathy called twillies smacked at Tim,
Who felt Tom's pain. It modulated soon
Into gemellar warmth, warming the grim
Venetian night with no Venetian moon.
In Brian's agent's twang, let's tike a pause 'ere
While the twins dare the choppy water's nausea.

For me, I face a fresh prosodic duty.
Rhyme for a time must be quadruple-barrelled
As well as treble. The occluded beauty
Of winter Venice, bilious-sea-apparelled,
Calls me to try on Byron's other suit. He
Used the nine-fingered stanza in *Childe Harold*,
Borrowing it from Spenser's *Faerie Queene*.
I'll rest before I ride that time machine.

THREE

'How is it?' Tim enquired as they both got
Into the *motoscafo* rocking rocking.
'Oh, androblastomas and God knows what.
The elevation of the plasma – shocking.
There's seminomas, teratomas blocking
The seminiferous ducts. The Leyding cell
Or the Sertoli cell or something.' Mocking,
He grimly grinned. And Tim said: 'I can tell
It hurts like bloody hell.' 'It hurts like bloody hell.

'Still, they'll soon have it off, with me reduced
To the fat squeaking eunuch of Stamboul
Or somewhere. How can no-balled me get used
To being seedless as a bloody mule
Or blasted bullock? The heaven-hailing tool
Diminished to a lowly waterspout,
The drying up of our genetic pool
Stagemanaged by that polycarpic lout
Who's doubtless left bastard breeders enough about.'

Tim would say nothing of the *vita nuova*
Envisaged for himself. Best to keep mum.
With gloom referred he let his eyes look over
The grey lagoonscape, very winter-glum,
Lights on the Grand Canal and lights on some
Brisk oriental shipping's horny fuss.
'We're staying with – Giudecca, here we come –
A woman writer, quite notorious.
Sex is her line. Ironical for both of us.'

'How?' A long island, shops and *trattorie*,
Casette undetached. They crashed its side.
A carious baroque church. The landing quay, a
Reserve for *vaporetti*, was denied
To their spark-puffing Charon. Thomas cried
Over the gale: 'I once gave her a hand
In Strasbourg as her francophonic guide
At a book-signing. She was grateful and
Said "Any time".' They climbed to dry or wettish land.

'She lives here?' 'There's some Yank organisation
That owns the place and lets it out to writers.
She's working on a novel, its location
Unserene Serenissima. Quite bright as
Pop-writers go. Nice of her to invite us.
Delighted when I told her you're a priest.
There's an unfrocked one in her book. You might as
Well tell her how God chains the sexual beast
Or vice versa. Buys a night's repose at least.'

'The Congress doesn't run to a hotel?'
'*Run from* was the procedure I employed.
When you've delivered better get the hell
Out. The dear delegates – needful to avoid
The swine when they're off duty. Overjoyed
They'll not be with your thesis. There'll be raps you'll
Not relish. Christ, the French will be annoyed.
Latin – it yearns to turn to French. Perhaps you'll
Be knifed. This bloody awful pain.' He took a capsule.

Timothy knew himself to be among
The world's last Latinists. But, all the same,
The resurrection of the Roman tongue
As Europe's lingua franca, with the name
Of Novolatin, was his aim. 'A game,'
Tom said, 'beyond the EEC's mentality.'
'Still, I propose it, and that's why I came.
Also the fee has its own mild reality.'
'Fare and and food only. Priests should be above venality.'

Their hostess was Rayne Waters, Tim was told.
He knew the name, had even seen her picture
(Blonde, hungry, about forty-five years old).
A parish girl had said: 'See how she's pricked your
Progenitive balloons and also kicked your
Male chauvinism' (*Not* mine') 'in the balls.'
A pert young miss. 'Your sacerdotal strictures
Are pissy slogans daubed on shithouse walls.
Up all your costive arses, starting with St Paul's.'

That girl had been much moved by Mistress Waters,
Whose novels answered Freud's frustrated whine
About what women wanted. All Eve's daughters
Now knew what women wanted – to decline
Sex as pure thrust. Sex they must redefine
As clitoral ecstasy, best with a vibrator,
Neck of a bottle of expensive wine,
Even a male as slavish excitator,
Coolly and fully used, coldly discarded later.

The lady, trousered, tall, came to the door
When Tom had knocked her knocker. She said: 'Hi.'
'A thing,' Tim teased, 'I didn't know before –
You're an Armenian.' 'Me Armenian? Why?'
'*Hai* is Armenian for Armenian.' 'I
Had to invite two eggheads for my sins.
Come in,' she said, 'and get your asses dry.
Jesus, but you're identical as pins.
Right, that's the epitaph for special brands of twins.'

'Epithet,' murmured Tim, but 'Epitaph,'
Tom nodded twice, 'for twins of a different sort.
Right, right.' She pealed a sympathetic laugh,
Well knowing what impended in his thought,
Or rather not impended, while Tim caught
In the old furnishings a dusty whiff
Of Unamerica. Clanking, she brought
America right in: martinis, stiff,
Probes for the teeth and for the brain a buoyant biff.

'We can defer our homage to Bellini'
(That mixture of Spumante and crushed peach)
'Until we eat our meatballs and linguini.
Well, well.' She lounged and looked from each to each.
'Were those nine fingers fixed so as to teach
Folk how to tell one brother from the other?'
She gave a tiny self-excusing screech
(An indiscretion droll eyes tried to smother.)
'Nature did this,' Tim said, 'our dear considerate mother.'

'When?' she asked Tom. 'We have to finish first
This nonsense that I had to organise
So that some Eurocash could be disbursed.'
'Why not to me?' growled Tim. 'An exercise
In nothing, then a nothing I disguise
As homage to the European mind.'
'You've had this Eurocrap up to your eyes,'
She said, 'Real Euroculture's what you find
In Eurodisneyland. Better if you resigned.'

'Homage?' Tim frowned. 'Next Wednesday the *Musée*
In Strasbourg, with my help, is to parade,
With all the medial bullshit of the day,
A kind of ideational cavalcade,
Great Eurothinkers, visually displayed –
Dante, Descartes, Pascal, Rousseau, Kant, Nietzsche,
Others. The academics have put paid
To my quite mild entreaty that they feature
Bill Shakes. They shook their beards. Hardly a Euroteacher.'

'This Muslim rage at anti-Muslim Dante,
Starting in Bradford – don't say you've not heard.
It's spreading.' 'Yorkshire news is pretty scanty
In Strasbourg. No, I haven't heard a word.
Jesus,' he yelled. The sleeping crab had stirred.
'I'll gulp my pills and get to bed.' 'Eat first.'
'Funny, the stab's moved upstairs. A referred
Pain, like a bloody boil that wants to burst.
O Jesus Christ,' he prayed. 'O Jesus Christ,' he cursed.

And so he knocked himself out for the night,
And Tim and Mistress Waters supped alone.
'So you're a priest.' Tim munched and said: 'That's right.'
Afar, Tom snored after a final groan.
'The ball-less twins.' She used a bantering tone.
'We're different, for my celibacy's just
A thing that I elected on my own.
Part of the priestly package that I must
Regard as a technique for overcoming lust.'

'Lust? Can a priest feel lust?' 'That's the whole point.
Lust racks and rends on every corporal level,
Burrows through bone and jumps in every joint,
A slavering incarnation of the devil.'
Tim was enjoying this. 'Lust can dishevel
The well-coiffed locks of faith.' Her eyes were wide.
'A good priest groans at the dysphonic revel,
Then grins. He's supersensually satisfied,
Until the time comes for the next satanicide.

'Mind if I smoke?' 'I do. Smoking's a sin.'
'Sin's focus has been changed.' Tim rudely flicked
His lighter, lighted, drew the sweet smoke in.
'Thou shalt not smoke,' he mocked, and then he nicked
The burnt end off. 'That's insolent.' She kicked
Him under the table. 'And thou shalt instead
Cosset the ecology, and interdict
All interdictions on raw sex,' he said.
'That was delicious. Now I'd better go to bed.'

The bedroom that she opened up for him
Was chill, austere, its odour monkish-cellish.
The ceiling though had flaking cherubim,
A noseless Venus. These failed to embellish
The narrow bed with any sensual relish.
He lay in threadbare sheets, untouched by fear
Of what might come. (Tom's snore, next door, was hellish.)
He knew she would pursue research in here.
Tim had confessed some writers in his long career.

He'd even, on a long-dead eve of Christmas,
Confessed the dubious Catholic Graham Greene.
He recognised him through his rhotacismus.
The sins were quite conventionally unclean,
Though glamourised by an exotic scene.
Tim hurled inordinate penance through the dark.
Evelyn Waugh's transgressions though had been
Mere scruples, Tim was saddened to remark.
It was too late to hear the sins of Muriel Spark.

He kept the light on. When she padded in,
La Waters, not la Spark, he grinned and nodded.
Her strawy hair was loose, she diet-thin
But, on the whole, quite curvilinear-bodied,
High-bosomed and firm-buttocked. Flaccid-rodded,
He lay beneath her. There was hardly room
For lateral lying. Fingers sharply prodded;
Her skin diffused a faint (*Rive Gauche*) perfume.
'Hardly a compliment.' 'A compliment to whom?'

'To you – a substance that I hardly know,
Or to generic woman? I'm for use
Remote from amatory – isn't that so?
Something to pump up your creative juice.
Arousal of the nerves. Stale clichés – loose
Tresses and looser lips. Should I be flattered?
Your heroine, I take it, must seduce
A priest and laugh to see his semen spattered.
Heaven versus woman, heaven's legions scattered.

'Love is the answer, love – you know the term?
The body sacramental to the soul.
No automatic spurt of neutral sperm.
My nerves are well excited, on the whole.
The context's masturbatory, your role
A stereoscopic centrefold. And mine?
A stereotypical cleric. If your goal
Is pinning me on pages, I decline.'
'All I could want,' she lied. 'OK, you're doing fine.'

'You're pinned already, *father*. Highly laudable,
Your attitude.' She jerked her long legs out,
The wirebrush pubic skirr just about audible.
She stood there, blazing naked, and her pout
Belied what her few crisp words were about.
'Besides,' he said, 'my brain's suffused with Latin.
Tomorrow's session.' 'Yeah,' she said, 'no doubt.
And what is "lust" in Latin?' Getting that in,
She got out angrily, but first she let a cat in.

The cat, Venetian, gravid, tortoiseshell,
As clouds with rain, swollen, ready to shed
Her kitten-load, uttered an urgent yell,
Disputing his possession of the bed.
Tim gave her room, she leapt. The Church still said
That sex meant progeny. This beast, concurring,
While Tim, tired, joined the temporary dead,
Parturiated in the dark, conferring
New life on Venice, waking Tim with deafening purring.

The blindlings pressed and sucked and Tim arose,
Found the disordered kitchen and there tapped
Its slim resources. Milk spilled on bare toes.
Six, seven, he counted, while the mother lapped.
He watched benignly, blessing, sitting wrapped
In his old dressing gown. Thus, to be freed
For sex meant being genitively trapped.
The mother leapt, her brood resumed its feed.
No freedom, taught that damned and dour Genevan creed.

At sun-up Tim woke Tom. Tom's brain was furred
But pain greatly diminished. Tim selected
A suit of decent grey. Their hostess stirred,
But only in her sleep. 'She's disaffected.
Europe, except as décor, is rejected,'
Tom said. His pain was grumbling. Tim was deft
At boiling eggs and coffee. They inspected
Venetian winter morning, sun-bereft,
Collected bags and left a thank-you note, then left.

'The last day, God be thanked,' Tom said. 'Your flight's
At three. At half-past five I hit the road.
I've no throat for the fishbones of tonight's
Dinner at Mestre.' Winter Venice showed
Small glamour. Here a belching steamer towed
A garbage barge. And there their talking shop,
San Giorgio, Euro-rented, dully glowed
In baroque honey from its mastoid top
To its canal-girt base: one *vaporetto* stop.

Across the Grand Canal imposed St Mark's
With desolate pigeons. Venice, Tim was thinking,
A gift to man from prudent politarchs
Who, sick of Attila, Italia's shrinking
From landlocked ruffians, ordained the sinking
Of piles to bear a city, while the Hun,
Boatless and huddled in his mareskin, stinking
Of mareflesh, squinted at its rising sun,
Wondering at a wonder. No Hun writ there could run.

Once did she hold the glorious East in. What
Had fleaed the lion's rump and pared his claws?
Pollution flowed from Mestre. She was not
The queen she had been. Ruskin had to pause
When writing *Fors Clavigera* because
Sickened by vapour from the *vaporetto*.
Decay came early. What were the seven laws,
Time's ruin? Shylock loosed from his *borghetto*
The plague. All else was for Canale Canaletto.

In the palazzo (Marble? Travertine?)
The Eurodelegates, sent here to measure
Limits of Euroculture, which was seen
By Frenchmen as a pure Cartesian treasure,
Saw Tom and Tim with no apparent pleasure.
Twinhood. A British trick. Some catch in it.
Tom took the chair. Tim, at his urbane leisure,
Tried wooing them with self-abasing wit,
Most stonily received. Tom winced. His twinges bit.

Our Roman heritage (Not ours – the Huns'),
Everything renderable (Megabytes?
Jets? Hamburgers?) The French discharged their guns
With 'French is Latin'. 'English claims no right
To be more than the dialect of flight,'
Tim said. 'I say this as an anglophone.
Mater Aeterna nostra – Latin.' 'Quite,'
A fellow-priest said. 'Kick the pope,' a lone
Red Ulsterman proclaimed. Tom gave a ghastly groan.

Tom tumbled from the chairman's chair he sat in,
Dead out. The session was dissolved. Tim bent,
Concerned. *'Eheu'*, he said in Novolatin.
He palped Tom's belly. Tom at once gave vent
To echo-rousing screams. Tim swiftly went
To a Titian beauty *in vestibulo.*
'*Subito* – get an *ambulanza* sent.
Un'emergenza. Il telefono.'
A Frenchman pushed him. 'You will know the *numero.'*

The ambulance was rather slow to come.
It came at last, not ambulant but biting
Foul water. Tom lay, breathing still but dumb.
A coffee klatsch found his near-corpse exciting.
Two orderlies in white, politely fighting
Through with a stretcher, joltingly then bore
Tom to the landing stage, first though inviting
Tim to embark. A loud ironic roar
Of *'Vale, fratres'* rang from Euroswine on shore.

Poor Tom saw nothing of the Grand Canal,
Palazzi, scafi, Peggy Guggenheim,
Caffè, alberghi, Harry's Bar et al.
They chugged past the Rialto, fighting time,
And reached at length the *ospedale.* 'I'm
Done for,' Tom gasped, as the few crewmen got
Grips on him for the lurching shoreward climb,
'Amen,' a gust of sempiternal rot
Gushed from the depths. 'Oh no,' Tim countergasped, 'you're
                                         not.'

Tim waited long among the whirring skirts
Of nursing nuns, with baggage at his feet.
Padre he called himself (it never hurts
To pull one's rank). He soured the air with sweet
Pulls at a rank cheroot, then stood to greet
White gravity. *'Dottore, che cos'è?'*
'Appendicite, padre.' Two discrete
Agonies, simultaneously at play.
Could one knife cut the two appendages away?

'Posso vederlo?' *'Certo.'* Tim was led
To where pyjama'd Tom lay part-sedated
Under a cross and in a narrow bed.
'Listen,' he breathed. 'It grieves me that you're fated
To do my job in Strasbourg.' Unelated,
Tim nodded. 'Ring Claudine. I have at home a
Young girl in hiding. Who'll explain.' Tim waited.
'The keys are in my bag.' He sank to coma
Then surfaced. 'My car's parked on the Piazzetta Roma.'

Tim blessed his brother. A preoperative
Trolley was trundling. Tom had ample cash,
Lire and francs in jacket pocket. Give
Name, phone, address. A nun with faint moustache,
Almoner, wrote. A girl in hiding? Rash,
He always had been. Puzzled, Tim now let a
Sospiro out. He saw a *scafo* splash
In at his summons. Boarded. *La Piazzetta*.
Better to take the road by day. Considerably better.

He landed, paid, then sought Tom's grey Mercedes,
Saying a sour goodbye to the Adriatic.
Across the way the Serbs were playing Hades
With ethnic cleansing. Only a fanatic
Could dream of Euro-unity. Erratic
That dream of Latin as a unifier.
I come to bring not peace but. Poets, vatic,
Knew all about the ever-widening gyre.
Tim found the car. It had a flabby offside tyre.

He opened, entered, switched on the ignition,
Eased out and scraped a rather dirty Fiat.
A left-hand drive. The left-hand door partition
Held maps. Mestre. Verona. He could be at
Milan by nightfall. Nothing much to see at
Milan. Ticino next. What must he do
At Strasbourg? First of all, insert the key at
Numéro neuf, rue Halévy. But who
Was this damned girl? Claudine, of course, he knew.

Claudine, Tom's colleague, was a tall and willowy
Alsacienne he'd met with Tom in Rome,
A classic blonde, superbly bosomed, pillowy,
Her long locks unsubmissive to the comb,
Divorcing at that time a sort of gnome
Of Zürich. Why did goddesses select
Models of ugliness to build a home?
Foils to their beauty? Tim could half-detect
Unpriestly urgings, though modified by respect.

Civilisation rayed out of Claudine,
Sweet Venus black-gowned as a polymath.
Not like that – Tim felt terribly unclean:
At Strasbourg he would have to take a bath.
He wondered was it really true: Hell hath
No fury like a woman sc— His hide
Crimped paperishly. Keep out of her path.
He and a Eurotruck failed to collide.
Old habit drove him to the wrong, or British, side.

Now concentrate. Check gas, oil, air and water as
You get geared to the Continental mode
(Napoleon and his tramping blueclad slaughterers
Monopolised the left half of the road).
The sky by turns hailed, drizzled, grinned and snowed,
Celestial dandruff really. By Piacenza
Mist fingered and the speeding foglamps glowed,
And all through Lombardy the fog grew denser.
Let him drive on. Meet him three frontiers hence, a
Reunion with Ariosto too. My dried-up pen, sir,
Madam, gladly dispenses with that brief spell of Spenser.

FOUR

So, after Agip service, fog, rain, snow,
Much-broken naps curled up on the rear seat,
Tim reached the Rhine, like Siegfried, though with no
Horn-blasts, only the monosonic bleat
Of Tom's befouled Mercedes. Where to go?
Foredawn. The syntax of the one-way street
Abusable through lack of traffic flow.
In searching for the place that Tom called home,
He met the Gothic *cathédrale* or *Dom*.

Should I correct that stanza? As you see,
It has an extra line and rhymes too much.
Curious, rather, wouldn't you agree?
– The way mild Spenser holds one in his clutch.
I quit his rhyme-scheme with a certain glee
But find it hard to disengage his touch,
Though I'm no longer drawn to his hexameters.
Rechain me, Ariosto's verse parameters.

Strasbourg, the Eurolawbox, much contested
Town of two cultures, Gallic and Teutonic.
The Germans had consistently been bested,
Though *Baekeoffe* and *Kougelhopf* were chronic
Items of the cuisine, where also nested
Choucroute garnie. Tim nodded at a sonic
Confusion from the coffee-serving wench,
Who, saying *Danke*, said it in *echt* French.

But *donc* she pointed out rue Halévy.
He parked and peered, had trouble with the lock.
Someone within was quicker than the key
And opened up. It would have been a shock
To see what he was now compelled to see
Had he not (nerves, as now, right as a rock)
Had that Venetian visit, though more crude
Or lewd: an adult female in the nude.

'Oh Tom, thank Christ you're here.' And she embraced him,
Debagging him as he put down his bag.
The light was dim and dawnish. As she faced him
He saw she was no man-exploiting hag
But young, bewildered. Pity then encased him
As she decased him of his inmost rag.
'Oh Tom, I've shivered all the fucking night,
And when I've dropped off waked with fucking fright.'

This was no time for stating his identity
Any more than when hearing a confession.
She dragged him to the bedroom, a male entity
She thought she knew, and he had the impression
It was sheer warmth she wanted. As he lent it, he
Felt in the stimulation of the flesh an
Untoward sense of holiness hold sway,
Like Flaubert's Julien l'Hospitalier.

But this girl was no leper, merely bruised
And shocked, and her right hand was bandage-bound,
Young, British (why?), and bodily abused,
Although her sexual appetite seemed sound.
She sighed, he warmed her, but as yet refused
Erotic contact. Her left fingers found
His scrotum, and she cried, as well she might,
'Oh Jesus Christ, they've put the bugger right.'

So 'Listen,' he said kindly. 'Merely listen.
I'm Tim, not Tom. Tom's being operated
On, now, in Venice. Please consider this an
Innocent swap. We're one. We emanated
From the same egg. One thing he has I miss – an
Annular digit – feel. It's compensated
By what poor Tom has forfeited – the status
Of owner of a full-fledged apparatus.'

She counted calmly. 'Tell me – who are you?'
'That means we've fifteen fingers altogether.
I'm Angela De'ath.' 'How do you do?'
Each introduced to each, he wondered whether
Their total nakedness was somewhat too
Intime for shaking hands beneath the feather-
Stuffed duvet. Still, they knew now who they were.
Tom sought a brief biography from her.

'I'm one of those enrolled in fucking CHAOS,
One of the mercenaries who save the sum
Of things for pay for anyone who'll pay us.
From Beirut, Ulster, Italy, I've come
Rhinewards. The swine are tough. They say *obey us*.
CHAOS – an acronym – Consortium
For Hastening the Annihilation of
Organised Soc – ' 'All in the name of love.

'I know the bloody business. So you maim
Yourself with an ill-handled hand grenade
Meant for some innocent, in the bloody name
Of bloody love. Some loveless bastard paid
To kill poor bastards. Supersessive shame
Or pain or fear or shock or something made
You see the evil. What's your origin?
Where are you from? How did this shit begin?'

She howled and clung to him. 'They ran away,
The swine. Tom found me bleeding in the dark,
Got me to hospital, came every day.
Tom's good. He'll get me home to Belsize Park
When I get better, book my flight and pay.'
'So no more love?' Tim's crabbed acerb remark
Made her howl worse. 'It's,' as her eyeballs flooded,
'Those bloody books on anarchy I studied.

'Love me, for God's sake, give me proper love.'
Well, here it was. Compassion mixed with rage,
A soupçon of contempt, all bade him shove
Priestly misgivings and the shame of age
Into the dark. Then a bedraggled dove,
No paraclete, flew from its unclean cage
And let its liquid siftings drip on him,
Clean Timothy aghast at filthy Tim.

Where did one draw the line? Pity will serve:
It often tastes like love. And briny kisses,
Pressed breasts, stroked thighs, probed anus, twitching nerve
Of frantic glans, cardiac frenzy – this is
Venerean heat a cold brain can observe –
A bestial barrage of blatant blisses,
The satyr mad to saturate the nymph
With exudations of ecstatic lymph.

They came, with morning, saw each other clearly –
On her bruised lips and unwashed hair, in him
A duplicate of Tom, or very nearly.
Chaos – no longer a mere acronym
But a too apt description of what really
Was female fetor – cup with bloody rim,
Canned slop half-eaten, hairballs and smoked butts
Confirmed that girls were fornicating sluts.

This naked bridges-burnt-behind-him man
Surveyed Tom's kitchen, gagging at the mess.
But then his thoughts more charitably ran
To pitying the slut's one-handedness.
Rhine water rattled in the one clean pan.
He called out 'Coffee?' She called back a yes.
At least there was some bread, a slice at most, a
Raw rusk that would grow ruskier in the toaster.

He donned his dressing gown. The telephone
Burred Frenchly. Foul enough Tom's bookish den
But masculinely so. With a faint groan
He watched a planet swim into his ken,
Raying responsibilities. The tone
Of Claudine's voice was querulous. Again
He summed up what the circumstances were.
She summoned a commendable *froideur*.

The exposition of great European
Contributors to European thought
Was ready, and tomorrow there would be an
Official opening. Tim as Tom now ought
To schlepp his ass (astonished, Tim could see an
American vulgarian had taught
Her showbizspeak) pronto to the *Musée*
In the Place Kléber. 'See you there. *Oqué?*'

But 'Food,' Angela pleaded. 'Give me food,
But give me love first, then a cigarette.'
Though this command opposed his present mood,
Tim, for his manhood's sake, was forced to get
Into his former posture and renewed
The warm tonalities of their duet.
He gave her coffee and a small cigar
And realised how friable men are.

He dressed and sought the nearest supermarket,
Sensing that Tom's Mercedes was familiar
To two blond louts who frowned and watched him park it.
He shrugged, then shivered, for the air was chilly, a
Rawish wind blew, Germanically stark. It
Was warm enough within. Taped muzak, sillier
Than was appropriate to the French mentality,
Twanged transatlantic Christmassy banality.

He piled his purchases in a wire basket –
Canned food, some grammes of *beurre*, two steaks to grill,
Beefeater gin, *baguettes* – the sort of task it
Had been his dour housekeeper's to fulfil.
New Beaujolais sulked in a plastic flask – it
Seemed evident the European will
Had yielded to some gross anonymous
Being, omnipotent, ubiquitous.

He paid and left, half-conscious as he drove
That he was being followed by a kind of
Ancient Lambretta, coughing as it wove
Between the petulant liverish cars behind. Of
Course, it was pure illusion. As Tim clove
The traffic, he was strangely put in mind of
One he had once confessed, a man who'd built
A world of helmeted emissaries of guilt.

So he got back and found her out of bed,
Thank God, in filthy T-shirt and torn jeans.
'Here's *déjeuner*, hardly *petit*,' he said,
Grilling the steaks and heating Boston beans.
He cut for her. She blubbered as she fed:
'A one-pawed hag still in her bloody teens.'
'How old exactly?' Tim asked as he sliced.
'Just gone sixteen.' (O Jesus bloody Christ.)

And bloody Tom. Yes, blood. Tim realised
He hadn't phoned. He phoned. Tom had been cut,
Appendix also testicle excised.
C'erano complicazioni, but
He'd live. Plenty of bed-rest was advised.
Full-fed and purring smoke, the green-eyed slut
Wished love as a dessert. Tim, somewhat sickly,
Drained gin and said it had to be done quickly.

The new museum, a converted warehouse,
Off Place Kléber, near the Librairie Fnac,
Was a grey brooding squarish, not quite square, house.
Tim frowned then shrugged. Its blunt and brutal lack
Of elegance was neither here nor there. HOUSE
OF EUROCULTURE blared, white upon black,
In French, of course. A structure hard to love.
Tim entered with his left hand in a glove.

Elegance was within – a massive hall
With nacreous lights and statues of the great,
Plastic, deplorable, but ten feet tall,
Forged by some hireling of the Eurostate
Who'd worked in films. Robed Dante led them all,
Beaked by the entrance, there to indicate
A sign: *'Speranza'* – hope – *'voi che entrate.'*
Tom cunningly had cut out the *lasciate*.

You dialled to hear Tom, prerecorded, say
'Cogito ergo sum' or 'God is dead',
And there were books and pictures on display,
Brisk commentaries on what these men had said,
And barks about their pertinence to today.
'We know' – green light that shook – 'more than the dead,
But it's the dead we know' – like greengage jelly. At
Least Tom had sneaked in something by Tom Eliot.

Claudine swished up, lean legs, flame hair, green eyes,
Unready to rebuke Tim's being late
(He gave no reason). Tim's fraternal guise
Was God's own blessing. 'Enemies await
Tom's absence', or, to transatlanticise,
'Too many top guys kicking ass. It's great
You're here. I guess they'll all be too damn dumb
To spot the difference, stoopid as they come.'

'Where did you learn to speak like that?' he asked.
'Rayne Waters said my English was too formal.'
(O Jesus Christ.) Tim gulped and quietly basked
In a blonde beauty that was supranormal.
Lust, for the time, was thoroughly decasked,
Nay drained, thus granting space to nourish warm al-
Ert desire to know, not to possess.
'Let's have a drink,' he said, and she said yes.

A drink was Pernod in a back *bureau*.
Tom's situation was, it seemed, precarious.
His British irony was growing so
Ironical that all the multifarious
Top functionaries wanted him to go,
Finding his epigrams less than hilarious.
Some grousers at the bureaucratic pinnacle
Thought that his attitudes were over-cynical.

And, an occasion for the grossest humour,
An imputation of his null virility
Had swollen here to far more than a rumour,
A total intellectual debility
Associated with a scrotal tumour.
All this, she sneered, was crass male imbecility,
The kind of diabolic grace that falls
On men whose brains are wholly in their balls.

That was the gist. Her exposition, Gallic,
Cartesian, was more rational and refined.
'When Tom returns,' Tim said, 'his lack of phallic
Endowment may well elevate his mind.
There'll be no outer change, even vocalic,
No elevation there, Tom reassigned,
Since his *vie sexuelle* is negative,
To the great tribe of those who think to live.'

'Can you assume his role – a month at least?'
'I have my own responsibilities.'
'You mean your function as a parish priest?'
'Well, no, no more. My late apostasy's
Ready to hatch, and the whole worldly feast
Is spread before me, meagre though it is.
Fresh steaming dishes bid me lift the lid,
Assuming too what Tom has forfeited.'

They looked each other in the eyes. Her blush
Dawned and then set. 'You two have known each other
How long?' A pause. 'I never wished to rush
Into a close relationship. Your brother
Was soaked in *Tristan* and proposed a lush
Liebestod for himself before the smother
Of the *élan vital* came in a fateful minute.
I told him no. I saw no future in it.'

'Where is your future?' 'There's no doubt it could
Have been with him, but I'm no Eloïse
To match his Abélard. I see no good
In popping passion into the deep freeze.'
'Two angels holding hands in bed. That would,'
Tim nodded, 'be a concept hard to seize
For anyone who's not been raised upon
Shelley's perverse *Epipsychidion*.'

'Tonight what are you doing?' asked Claudine.
'You need to eat. Why not come home with me?'
'I must work out a speech as well as clean
A dwelling much neglected. Still, *merci.
Demain peut-être?*', wondering if she'd been
Apprised of that young succuba. No, she
Had not, it seemed. She asked no question now.
'Demain, д'accorд.' They parted. *'Ciao.' 'Ciao.' 'Ciao.'*

He pierced the Strasbourg dusk and was surprised
To find that Tom's street door was open wide.
Someone had come — so much was advertised.
He parked with haste. With haste he ran inside.
She'd gone. A flash inside his brain advised
Now of a nexus — louts, pursuit. He cried
Aloud on the stupidity of youth, paced
Up and then down. He caught a whiff of toothpaste.

A message on the bathroom shaving glass —
THEYVE TAK — and then the flat tube's inanition.
Peppermint on the air. Alas, alas
For youth, for her. Some new disruptive mission.
Abduction. Pain. For God's sake let it pass.
Curing the postlapsarian condition
Was someone else's duty to fulfil,
And the damned girl was gifted with free will.

Clean up, clear up, erase, try to restore
Scholarly order, meaning tolerated
Disorder. Let the ancient Hoover's roar
Rampage, and let black plastic bags inflated
With rubbish rubbish sulk outside the door.
He mopped the kitchen and then dissipated
With *Fleurs des Forêts* an old stench of fish (an
Odour devised by some devout technician).

114

So then a supper of canned *bisque*, torn bread,
Gin and a Schimmelpenninck, while he wrote
A note or so. And then he went to bed.
He had not changed the sheets. A whiff of goat,
Female arousal, sperm-spill, blood-gouts, shed
A pagan benison. And so to float
Off to a noon of rank Sicilian charm, pits
And flesh of peaches, fauns scratching their armpits.

Or Irish oxters, Oxtail University,
Course in French letters with the great god Pan
Presiding, dribbling, mouthing. Then, oh curse it, he
Assumed the lineaments of a burnished man.
Seeds spilt like pennies from a great burst purse. City
Darkness and alley whispers, a split can
Of nameless effluent, the great black crack
Back of a sack of a slack zodiac.

Tim, late awake, had breakfast and a shave.
He rang up Dorothy, who'd just recorded
The morning's tale of infamy, from grave
Through gritty and grotesque to frankly sordid.
Tim gravely took it in and then he gave
His own sharp narrative. And, one word more, did
She know of the conclave that was advertised?
Yes, Brian rang. Brian was not surprised.

Next Tim, with some small difficulty, got
His curate, Father Benlowe, on the phone.
He had a problem. Oh? Precisely what?
A Pakistani girl, who'd not made known
Her wishes to her elders – she durst not –
Had come to see him, lateish and alone,
And shown a strong desire to be instructed
About the faith, eventually inducted.

115

'*Liberum arbitrium*,' Tim sighing said.
'Not even Muslim nonsense can deprive
The questing soul of that. Go right ahead.
But one who is Islamically alive
May not prefer to join the Christian dead.
Between the two of you you may contrive
To bring about a literal martyrdom,
But she can choose – *liberum arbitrium*.'

Michael Servetus, martyr, chose to swim
Into his brain. He stared at Tom's black blank
Computer screen, and it stared back at him.
Work beckoned, though the whole conception stank.
He freely willed to propagandise grim
Determinism. Money in the bank.
Free will perhaps was the destructive siren. He
Knew Calvinists would not perceive the irony.

But first things first. This opening first of all.
He chose a sober suit and tie and dressed.
His left hand bore a wool-stuffed fingerstall –
A whitlow, hangnail, something. For the rest,
Tim was pure Tom, though ready to appal
(That Venice failure still oppressed, depressed)
The non-Latinophones (in Francophonian
Allophones though) with something Ciceronian.

Driving the car, he mouthed his Latin loud.
He was on time. Claudine's bright loveliness
Irradiated a large subfusc crowd.
Here was the mayor. There, sour under duress,
The Eurodelegates. Tim bobbed and bowed
And, with Claudine, gold in a golden dress,
Elbowed and thrust, as through a football scrimmage,
To a rostrum under rostral Dante's image.

'*Urbis praefecte honorabilis*'
(Epithet used just once by Cicero),
'*Legati, nuntii*' (was that a hiss?),
'*Civites, vos salvere jubeo.*'
He got no further in his speech than this.
The bomb was deafening, a gleam, a glow,
Screams, shouts, collisions, runnings, eyes dilated,
Horrified howls. Dante disintegrated.

Tim grabbed Claudine sheer clear of the hit head;
A fingerless hand struck his, pure paint and plastic.
The cameras flailed. '*Les Musulmans*,' Tim said.
Some things cohered. Claudine's faint gasps and spastic
Shudders grew worse, while Dante's ruins shed
Odour of something apt, infernal. Drastic
Inquiries called for. Tim remembered now
Algerian doormen. That was wrong somehow.

Probably all this would be blamed on Tom.
Perfide Albion. Lawrence d'Arabie.
Tom-Tim should have nosed out that bloody bomb.
The Dante head frowned hard at him and he
Kicked it. It turned to filthy ash, wherefrom
Comminatory smoke rose. Tight-held she
Knew new distress. The mayor was loud and voluble.
Descartes shook, and the crowd grew highly soluble.

Descartes was merely shaky. Islam held
Nothing against him, knowing nothing of him.
'*Cette exposition est ouverte*,' Tim yelled
And bore Claudine away. The lights above him –
Nous connaissons les morts – spilled down and spelled
A quite dire message. Crowds began to shove him
And Claudine out, still tremulous, tremulous she,
And he a little with the ignition key.

Her deafness, unabated, worried most.
He drove her to Tom's dwelling, set her down,
Fed her some cognac. Then, a mixed-up host,
He changed the bedsheets, saw her golden gown
Was gritty, ashy; she, aghast, a ghost,
Wore pallid plaster as a comic crown.
A bath, a bed, or both, something to wear?
Tim shrank into a *bonhomme à tout faire*.

Later, in bathrobe, glowing, hair near dry,
She was no longer deaf. 'A childhood scare.
Italian Alps. *Caduta Massi.* I
Was six years old. A rock fell. A mere hair
Divided me from it. Such terrors lie
Awaiting wakening. It was like that there.
I'll sleep a little.' 'Do so. I'll prepare
Some broth.' She tottered bedwards, he elsewhere.

He mixed some gin and Pernod to reprove his
Shivering still. The TV news showed all.
Special effects, though, in disaster movies
Would have made more of it. So. What we call
Real life, in shifting to a fictive groove, is
Seen as inferior fiction. 'What's the fall
Of Dante,' Tim groused to his gin and Pernod,
'To a multimillion Hollywood *Inferno*?'

But then the news said that the Rhine police
Had grabbed three terrorists, two self-confessed
Tools of disruption, garnished with a piece
Of cinefootage. Just as Tim had guessed,
Angela featured, howling without cease
Though without sound: innocent, pushed, forced, pressed.
Her name, De'ath, meaning *La Mort*, was seen
As guilt enough, so said the *speakerine*.

118

Switch off, doze, wake, give the *bouton* a push, de-
Siring news of bigger worlds without.
The sex-life of ex-President George Bush, de-
Linquencies no one cared a bit about.
A failed West End assault on Salman Rushdie.
Islam again. A loud Koranic shout
From Teheran, an imperious demand
That Dante's works be mondially banned.

Tim felt uneasy. He'd as good as doffed
The Christian armour meet for holy war.
The secular hardware was over-soft.
Should tolerance meet intolerance? Once we bore
Paynim-defying banners high aloft.
The Christian West was rotten to the core,
A culture facing in its deliquescence
The rigour of a million stars and crescents.

She stirred, she yawned. The cupboard was near-bare.
Some onion soup? He looked in on Claudine.
She was awake and in her underwear.
'Better?' he gulped. 'Better.' He said he'd seen
The news. She nodded, gave him a green stare.
'One bed,' she said. 'Two people'. Gulp. 'You mean – ?'
He coughed, and in his pocket had to root am-
Ong used Kleenex to entrap the sputum.

He coughed and coughed and what he coughed was crimson.
Had Dante, pulverised, assailed a lung?
Phlegm deep encrimsoned. In his lower limbs an
Unwonted trembling started, so he clung
To the night table. The sheer sight of Tim's un-
Stanchable flow froze Claudine's eyes and tongue.
And then he stopped, but held on to his fright.
There'd be no casual dalliance tonight.

119

Claudine, quite clearly, did not care for sickness.
'Give me my dress, lend me a raincoat. I'll
Call for a taxi.' Tim surveyed the thickness
Of a haematic blob with a sour smile.
She dressed with an exemplary quickness.
'I'll drive you home.' But still he let her dial
The number with a panicky velocity.
'I hit a vein. Senescent varicosity.'

She left, like someone fleeing from *la peste*,
Abandoning poor Tim to soup and smoke.
He twirled a Schimmelpenninck. It was best
To let the bronchii rest and not provoke
Another crimson fit. He grew oppressed
By a conceit, a sort of holy joke:
To match the sinful seed that he had spent
Christ's blood streamed in the inner firmament.

The hound of heaven snuffled at his back.
He pissed white wine then gazed on his reflection.
Inveterate grey had swamped Yukari's black.
His eyes were glazed, his body a collection
Of bones grown brittle and of skin grown slack.
He hawked, spat in the bowl. A close inspection
Showed that Christ's blood or his had sidled off,
Permitting him a candid smoker's cough.

Rejuvenation? Never. Not a hope.
The wooing of Claudine by candleshine
While Strasbourg snow like fluffy shaving soap
Lay on the Tudor-looking roofs. Red wine
And smoking *Baekeoffe*. No grab, no grope,
Avoidance of a Casanovan line.
His need and hers. He watched *perhaps* collapse.
His teeth, he saw, had unattractive gaps.

He wondered: should he cry himself to sleep?
Thought better of it, downed some gin, soon snored,
Leaving it to the Strasbourg sky to weep,
Rose early, shopped, drove back. He had on board
Enough provisions, so he thought, to keep
A winter trapper. Reverently he poured
A sacramental malt, reverently sipped,
Then sat to process half a yard of script.

Start in the middle. Could Servetus be
The bloody villain Sewall had alleged?
Tim thought of Michael, Miguel, and could see
The poor boy in warm water, parent-pledged
To papal choir castration (of course, he
Had no say in the matter). The blunt-edged
Shears snipped potential manhood. Sexicide.
He'd sing soprano till the day he died.

But Miguel joined the medical fraternity,
And killed and cured throughout the whole Hispanic
Terrain, heaped gold, although he had to earn it. He
Was calm when plague made every province panic.
The rational approach – he had to learn it. He
Combined the syllogistic and organic,
And while to most the blood was merely bloody,
He made its logic his profoundest study.

Long before Harvey, Dr M. Servetus
Saw that the blood sustained an ordered motion.
Like earth itself, it had to circulate. As
Stream blossomed into river, river ocean,
And then through rainclouds back to streamy status,
So it. That cycle earned his full devotion.
Rejecting blood as a red static pillar, he
Pursued its course – artery, vein, capillary.

Of course, he played the earnest pedagogue,
Expanding though, for, to his own surprise,
A theological near-analogue
Forced him, alas, to sneer and stigmatise
The Trinity as a three-headed dog,
Meaning the orthodox concept – unwise –
Replacing it – three persons quite distinct
But, so to speak, haematically linked.

This to the old devout must seem strong meat.
The ultimate in heaven was not stasis
But motion. God rendered himself complete
Through filiality, incarnate basis
Of a kinetic stuff, the paraclete
The network where eternal change takes place. Is
Not this, thought Tim, although it warmed his heart, a
Vision most apt for a prospective martyr?

Servetus published his *De Trinitate*.
Both Rome and Wittenburg emitted thunder;
Zwinglians, Hussites tore the work apart. He
Tried to contend the text expressed a wonder:
Essential three in one. God's subtle art. He
Showed his true oneness manifested under
Mere outward show: call that the Holy Trinity,
Himself the blood, the cyclical divinity.

So Tim interpreted the doctrine. Though
He could not well remember what he'd read,
He well recalled how Miguel had to go
From land to land to land to beg his bread
And save his body from the burning, so
Finally trod where it was death to tread,
Seeking the hagiocracy where faith
Was logic, not a mythopathic wraith.

He landed in Geneva. To his inn
A state official bearing a white rod
Came right away, announcing with a grin
That the Genevan state, body of God,
Arrested him. Here secular crime and sin
Were one. The official used his rod to prod
The victim: he must go at once to state
Incarceration and a lengthy wait.

The gaol was filthy, and the leering warders
Derided his soprano squeak. They saw
His ball-less groin and roared, obeying orders
To check that peccative, or papist, flaw.
Then came a long procession of recorders
Recording what incensed Genevan law
Or theocratic doctrine. From the horse's
Mouth, or whinnying mare's, nightlong discourses.

Servetus met his judges. Honest John,
Or crafty Calvin, kept out of the way,
Although the judgment was his own. Upon
The teachings of that dwarf whose blood was whey,
Semen pure water, a phenomenon
Whose only beauty, so they tell us, lay
In an exemplary prose style, was based
The doled-out doom the shivering Spaniard faced.

The public burning was a fine diversion
To citizens deprived of basic joys.
Lausanne arranged a holiday excursion.
Black-suited bankers turned to boisterous boys
Remembering pre-Calvinist immersion
Into a brantub full of toys. The noise
Of 'Heretics to hell' was sweetly festive.
The wood was damp, though, and the crowd grew restive.

123

The flames leapt late. Servetus reeked of crackling
After his stuck-pig squeals. John Calvin shammed
Delicacy through absence, frowning, tackling
A riddle: why this damned one felt undamned,
Screaming to God, his skin scorched devil-black (Ling-
Ering, yes, shrieked fury) while red torment crammed
Each orifice, stink of an outraged God.
Yet it was God he called on. Very odd.

There was a Calvin problem, was there not?
God made his mind up, right from the beginning,
That some were damned, some saved, and strictly what
You did with life, saintly by choice or sinning,
Mattered to God not one benighted jot.
You prosper? That probably means you're winning.
You're losing, lost – the sudden voices shout it.
You're lost, and nothing can be done about it.

Conviction of damnation, so they tell,
Afflicted Calvin later. The good Lord's
Guerdon for faithful service? Fiery hell.
Well, no – no punishments and no rewards.
Servetus rose and his accuser fell?
That's all too possible, and it accords
With logic, justice being man's creation:
Its symbol is a public conflagration.

It would not do, the damned thing would not do.
And *homo fuge* sang from blood released
On one of Tom's white shirt cuffs. So it's you,
Truepenny. Then the sanguine spasm ceased.
Veins brittle in the throat – that might be true,
But something whispered of the encroaching beast.
Why should his twin be stricken and he not?
The dart was blind: it fired at any spot.

A doctor. Who? Well, possibly Denise's?
That gush of red, though, had been alienating.
He'd wait for Tom's return and help to ease his
Way into eunuchdom. Life was all waiting,
N'est-ce pas? Nicht wahr? But still it didn't please his
Habit of priestly pressure (fulminating:
'Give up that sin that eats you to the quick!')
Delay, and you confirmed that you were sick.

This was a case where languages looked in.
A foreign tongue bestowed an A-effect:
Somebody else had the disease, or sin –
Lust or leukaemia. In this respect
The surgery and confessional were akin.
When Christ spoke to the lost and the elect,
He'd have to, Tim supposed, be polyglot.
One's mother tongue spoke true, the others not.

And so he'd wait until he'd winged his way
Back to the warm vernacular, GPs
With common colds and common phonemes, grey
Worn suits and cardigans, and Melanese
Receptionists, and no damned fees to pay.
He was entitled to a large disease:
He'd made his dogged weekly contribution
To the decaying liberal institution.

And now he thought he'd better telephone
To Brian's agent. After 'Can I 'elp
Yew?' and a rasping nailfile, he made known
His summary rejection. A foul yelp
Of Cockney execration in a tone
Apt for a brawl ensued. The unwiped whelp,
The moneyloving lout, could not conceive a
Conscience. So Tim down-slammed the damned receiver.

He cooked, drank, smoked a little, roamed the city
In snow or slush or rain. The *tussis* racked him
Hardly at all. A lone week. Neither pity
Nor friendship gave Claudine cause to contact him.
He spent long hours in the cathedral, pretty
Well reconciled to going back to black. Tim
Saw the priest's duties now as purely formal,
A trade a trade, the situation normal.

And yet – the fantasy applied to Thomas
Rather than Timothy – if only God
Would grant a sign – no need for stops and commas –
Some hieroglyph, graffito, half-baked clod
Of cuneiform-marked clay, an ill-aimed bomb, a s-
Usurrus, fart, intrusion of the odd
Into the even mainstream of the day,
A prodigy. God didn't work that way.

He trudged back to Tom's place. The telephone
Was trilling to itself. He lifted it.
Tom's voice, assertive, male (the eunuch tone
Did not ensue when shears or scissors bit
Post-pubertally). 'Coming home. Alone?
No, no, accompanied. Feeling not too fit.
Weak rather. Hm. Don't think I like that cough.
Back Tuesday night. Then you can bugger off.'

Kind. Brotherly. Tim did not like it either.
He spat a rust-gout in his handkerchief.
Was he a little thinner? Oh well, by the
End of the week the dubious relief
Of solid knowledge. Then perhaps to die the
Death. An endless silence after a brief
Earth-sojourn. All the putative joys untasted.
Circular speculation. A life wasted.

The bed must now be Tom's. Tim's place of rest
Could be the armchair or the filthy floor.
Then off off (bugger). Fly. Change ticket. Best
Find out the worst in Manchester. Restore
Faith in the craft, leave unfaith unconfessed.
Stand up for Dante's faith, if nothing more.
Accept with glee the bells Holst tolls in 'Saturn',
Glad in a sense life can disclose a pattern.

'Hi,' jeered Rayne Waters. 'Ah. Armenian still.'
He might have guessed that she might be his brother's
Compagnon de voyage. More weak than ill,
Tom tottered bedwards. She displayed no mother's
Solicitude nor any nursing skill,
No *tenerezza*. Men were just The Others.
She dumped the ball-less Tom, then went away:
She'd other fish to fry or ploys to play.

Tim sat down by his brother. 'The girl's gone.
She went, was taken, played a minor part
In blowing up your Dante. She was on
The TV news. I saw her howl her heart
Out. Poor girl, poor child.' Tom turned upon
The muftied priest with 'Christ, you'd better start
Getting your pontiff to get furious.
This can't go on.' Tim said: 'It's up to us.'

Tom paused awhile, and then said: 'What's the view
Of Holy Bloody Mother Church about
Sapphic activities?' 'What's that to you?'
'Nothing directly. I must live without
Physical love, but what these lesbians do
Has some residual interest, no doubt.
Rayne Waters kindly offers, *sans pudeur*,
The washed-out pleasures of the mere *voyeur*.'

127

'With whom?' 'Why, can't you guess? Claudine, no less.'
Tim's heart might well have dropped at that disclosure.
Only his face fell. 'What a bloody mess,'
Tom groaned. 'You're clearly shocked. That only shows your
Innocence.' 'It's what women don't confess,'
Tim said. 'The theological exposure
Of non-productive sex cannot include
What women do in bed, however lewd.

'The only sexual sin is waste of seed,
And women clearly have no seed to spend.
Therefore the lesbian embrace is freed
From total censure. But the sexual end
Is several miles off Nature's simple need
– Viz. procreation. Hence we can't defend
Sapphism. It sits tentatively in
The book of law. Call it a venial sin.'

'Call it a damned perversion,' execrated
Tom. 'Life denial, voluntarily chosen.
It's only now that, detesticulated,
With my paternal promptings permafrozen,
I see, like poor Macbeth, an elongated
Procession, files and flanks and ranks and rows, an
Image of progeny now unfulfillable,
Time negative, breathless, down to the last syllable.'

'An animal fulfilment.' 'All we are.'
Tom sipped some Scotch. 'I leave you at first light.'
Tim downed unwanted gin, smoked a cigar,
Coughed, doused it, said: 'I think you'll be all right.
The larder's stocked, there's petrol in the car.'
And then: 'We can expect a lively night.
Christ and the Antichrist. I'll see you then.
Let's sleep now. Angels guard you, me. Amen.'

128

Tim, hurling back to London, left a coin
Of scarlet tribute in the toilet bowl.
He tubed to Green Park. Twinges in the groin
Bound him to Tom, but sordor in the soul
Was all his own. He shrugged and went to join
A brief confession queue at Farm Street, stole
Out of his past the trick of sincere penance,
Then in a pub toasted himself with Tennant's.

Yukari was alone. 'So. You come back.'
'Where's Dorothy?' 'Doloti she not here.
Leave you a letter.' 'Give me.' *I must attack*
This ghastly disbelief in hell, my dear
Timothy. Though I don't expect to pack
These village halls, just one retentive ear
Justifies slamming home the word believe.
I'll be back home just before Christmas Eve.'

And then they looked each other in the eyes
And Tim, in a slow rhythm, shook his head.
Temptation? Certainly. Therefore unwise
Even to snooze a half-hour on that bed.
'I go. I come again.' Formal goodbyes,
And then the tube to Euston. Coughed up red
Did not recur until the train reached Crewe.
In Manchester it was a flag. It flew.

Dr Mackenzie had Tim's chest x-rayed,
Then sent his inner portrait to the Royal
Infirmary, an appointment being made
With the great Dr Gogol, who was loyal
To cancer, his first love. He'd plied his trade
In Europe and on transatlantic soil.
His origin was Minsk or Pinsk or Moscow. Pe-
Rusing Tim's chart he called for a bronchoscopy.

129

Tim, somnolent, was raped via his nose
By tubes that told the truth about each lung.
The truth was far from welcome: in repose
After the process he was briskly stung
Awake by Gogol's waiting to disclose,
In a Slav version of Tim's native tongue,
A stern prognosis crassly negative:
Inoperable; say six months to live.

Tim now became a *Hermes psychopompos*,
Leaving the living to his loving curate
Who, as a guide to life, was still in rompers.
The sick and dying Tim must now assure, at
Any rate, that he too could encompass
Similar fears, despairs, also endure at
Much their own level what death had in store,
God being the great blackness, nothing more.

As for the Pakistani girl, the would-be
Convert, Tim found no hardship in dissuasion.
'I say these words, my child, for your own good. Be
What you have been and don't grant an occasion
For filicide, sororicide. It should be
Enough to live. The ultimate invasion
Of nothingness, by sword or scimitar,
Says, too late, *Lay off faith*. Stay as you are.'

Quantification. Quantification. Tim
Coughed blood. The whole world is our hospital,
Endowed by the ruined millionaire. The grim
Contractive nature of the interval
Did not exorbitantly trouble him.
We meet the real – axiomatical –
Sooner not later. It would be a rather
Strange Christmas gift, recovery of a father.

Tim told Tom nothing, but Tom sent a scrawl:
'Some nastiness, quite unanticipated
Since unanticipatable, for all
Nature must go against it. Terminated
At month's end job. Scandal, or what they call
A scandal. Once the great cantant castrated
Had sexual glamour. Difficult to conceive.
Sheer nonsense, really. See you Christmas Eve.'

FIVE

Christmas Eve morning, cold in the old style,
With even snow, a homage to Charles Dickens,
And Tim and his half-sister held their bile
Back, back: can art be art if it so sickens?
Their private preview, nearly half a mile
Of gallery, wrung them, like the necks of chickens.
This exhibition – what could one learn from it?
The diarrhoeal link of paint and vomit?

There was one theme, just one – corporeal outrage.
No skill in texture, no 'fag on at flesh'.
No teacher with a salutary clout, rage
At technical incompetence, no mesh
Of rules had tripped him, instilled wholesome doubt. Rage
Raged from the canvases, all strangely fresh,
And strangely gleeful, as if human pain
Were necessary bread. It was insane.

'It's hell,' cried Dorothy, as she surveyed
A sexual posture and three screaming faces.
'No, rather it's what leads to hell.' Tim made
A sickened gesture at some foul embraces
That, surely, sheer anatomy forbade,
Forbade. 'Bad, bad,' Tim groaned. 'There must be traces
Of him in us. God, are we really free
Or sick from birth with sap from the parent tree?'

They slithered to a pub he knew in Pimli-
Co. They could not eat. 'There's a rehearsal
This afternoon.' Tim downed his brandy grimly.
'He curses through the eye and now the curse'll
Come through the ear.' She sipped her sherry primly.
'It won't be Bach or Beethoven or Purcell,'
Tim said. 'There won't be any Christmas jollity.
But Brian said look in and taste the quality.'

He went alone. Brian, stern on the dais,
Rebuked a rather swollen LPO
(Eight horns, extra percussion). 'What you play is
Inferior to Beethoven, we know.
But, trumpets, your (bar twelve) sardonic bray is
Unwanted commentary. You all can show
Contempt a little later, over beer.
It's bad musicianship, you bastards, here.'

Strangely enough, the brief *Swiss Overture*
(Why that, for God's sake?) was a counterpart
To Tim's own feelings. Clockwork rhythms, pure
Calvin chorales on alpenhorns. Not art
(Civic commission?). Towards the end the dour
Texture slowed down to mock a thumping heart.
Whose? Then it broke. Was that Servetus yelling?
Music is only sound. There was no telling.

The bass trombone concerto – soloist
G. Gregson – seemed to speak rather than sing.
A strong dot-dash component braved a mist
Of mock Wagnerianism. Was the thing
Venturing on a message? The humorist,
Sardonic, very dry, in Byrne, let ring,
On four tuned cymbals and an anvil ding,
Inverted and reversed, 'God Save the King'.

136

Add a mixed chorus and percussion players
With instruments Tim had not seen before.
These slushed through darkest Africa. Foul layers
Of dissonance obscured a primal core
Of all too primal squalor. Conrad. Flay us,
Go on, tear off our hides. The heart of. More
Dissonance. More. Then – Mistah Kurtz he dead.
'A *Zigarettenpause*,' Brian said.

And so it went. Today's rehearsal ended
With music for an unfilmed *Time Machine*,
A suite that, mostly tonal, condescended
To populism. The Victorian scene
Was not derided, and the music tended
To teatime tenderness when earth had been
Denuded, slowed, reduced to tuba groans
With microtonal burps on five trombones.

The son had taken nothing from the father.
'Look at this score,' said Brian in the bar.
Tim peered at it. A symphony, or rather
A dysphony. 'You can see where you are –
Flutes top, bass bottom. See that midway lather
Of horns and trumpets. See? He's gone too far.
Too far. Take in that devastating chord – it has
Twenty-four different notes. God help our auditors.'

'Where is he? Where's he come from?' 'Came last night
With big black escort. Some quite vague location
Upon the Kalahari border. Quite
The tribal patriarch, due for immolation,
Entitled, though, to ask for death to smite
On his own birth-soil. No real new sensation
For Claridges. Our damned Hibernian jester meant
Nothing, I think, by a last will and testament.

'They speak a language there called !Ku or !Kung.'
(He scrawled the names in beer). 'Palatal stop,
That exclamation point. This Bushman tongue
Has just a hundred consonants – the top
Linguistic mondial phonemic rung.
Talk about riches in a rag-bone shop.
That's the twins' legacy. The other stuff
Is mine. Genetical amends. Enough.'

So, Christmas Eve – ah, bitter chill, etcetera.
The Mayfair trio kept the appointed date,
Tim dog-collared. Tom sent another letter, a-
Ssuring them that he'd be there, though late.
The darkling room where all the gathering met, a ro-
Coco misfit, not full, had many a plate
From which the reek of meat, coffined in bread,
Proclaimed that eating meant eating the dead.

The jugs of drink looked urinous, and smelt so.
Some oil lamps stank of human hair and soot.
The first arrivals, Brian said, had felt so
Crawsickened that they'd left. 'Mischief's afoot,'
Gagged Dorothy. 'Let the assembly melt so
That just the authentic residue stays put,'
Said Brian. 'All these brownskins here won't do,
Except the odd photographer or two.'

Now tetraphonic speakers spoke, or crackled.
'Christmas is jingling towards us. Santa
Claws at the reins. His reindeer, firmly shackled,
Snarl at each other, set then to a canter
Over the snow to Bethlehem,' they cackled.
'Maria wonders (birth-pangs start instanter)
What her place is within the scheme of things.
Music. She has her carol. Hark. She sings.'

In this spinning room,
Reduced to a common noun,
Swallowed by the giant belly of Eve,
The pentecostal sperm came hissing down.
Lullay lullay.

I was no one,
For I was anyone,
The grace and music easy to receive,
The patient engine of a stranger son.
Lullay lullay lullay.

His laughter was
Fermenting in the cell.
The worm, the fish was chuckling to achieve
The rose of the disguise he wears so well.
Lullay haha lullay.

And though by dispensation
Of the dove
My flesh is pardoned of its flesh, they leave
The rankling of a wrong and useless love.
Lullay.

Four blacks, vast, nearer seven feet than six,
Trampled the floor with corresponding weight,
Feet shod and capable of lethal kicks,
Cheaply smart-suited, the smooth-shaven pate
Of each agleam amid the candlesticks.
The hotel lights switched off, a sort of state
Of primitivity ensured a scare
Among the twenty-odd who waited there.

The fourfold voice resumed. 'That Yuletide carol
Was penned to lift your hearts and make you feel good.
Better to tap a celebratory barrel
And groan dyspeptically after your gross meal? Good.
I've figuratively donned the bard's apparel
To give five restive sonnets to John Gielgud,
Who'll read them now. They sum up all our annals
In five disjunctive but connective panels.'

I

Sick of the sycophantic singing, sick
Of every afternoon's compulsory games,
Sick of the little cliques of county names,
He bade the timebomb in his brain go tick
And tock. As binary arithmetic
Resentment spent its spleen. Divided aims
Meant only 2. But, quivering in flames,
He read: 'That flower is not for you to pick.'

Therefore he picked it. All things thawed to action,
Sound, colour. A shrill electric bell
Summoned the guard. He gathered up his faction,
Paused on the brink, thought, and created hell.
Light shimmered in miraculous refraction
As, like a bloody thunderbolt, he fell.

Bells clanged white Sunday in, a dressing-gowned day.
The childless couple basked in the central heat.
The comics came on time. The enormous meat
Sang in the oven. On thick carpets lay
Thin panther kittens, locked in clawless play.
Their loving flesh was O so firm, their feet
Uncalloused. Wine they drank was new and sweet.
Recorders, unaccompanied, crooned away.

Coiled on the rooftree, bored, inspired, their snake
Crowed in black Monday. A collar kissed the throat,
Clothes braced the body. A benignant ache
Lit up a tooth. The papers had a note:
His death may mean an empire is at stake.
Sunday and this were equally remote.

A dream, yes, but for everyone the same.
The thought that wove it never dropped a stitch.
The absolute was everybody's pitch,
For, when a note was struck, we knew its name.
That dark aborted any wish to tame
Waters that day might prove to be a ditch
But then were endless growling ocean, rich
In fish and heroes – till the dredgers came.

Wachet auf! A fretful dunghill cock
Flinted the noisy beacons through the shires.
A martin's nest clogged the cathedral clock,
But it was morning: birds could not be liars.
A key cleft rusty age in lock and lock.
Men shivered by a hundred kitchen fires.

They lit the sun and then their day began.
What prodigies that eye of light revealed,
What dusty parchment statutes they repealed,
Pulling up blinds and lifting every ban!
The galaxies revolving to their plan,
They made the conch, the coin, the cortex yield
Their keys, and, in a garden, once a field,
They hoisted up the statue of a man.

Of man, rather: to most it seemed a mirror;
They strained their necks with gazing in the air,
Proud of those stony eyes unglazed by terror.
Though marble is not glass, why should they care?
Eat now, and vomit later, the sweet error:
Someone was bound to find his portrait there.

Augustus on a guinea sat in state,
The sun no proper study, though each shaft
Of filtered light a column. Classic craft
Abhorred the arc or arch. To circulate
Blood or ideas meant pipes, and pipes were straight.
As loaves were gifts from Ceres when she laughed,
Thyrsis was Jack. Caruso on a raft
Sought Johnjack's rational island, loath to wait

Till sun, neglected, took revenge, so that
The columns nodded, melted, and were seen
As Gothic arches where a goddess sat.
It seemed then that a rational machine
Granted to all men by the technocrat
Was patented by Dr Guillotine.

The voice said. 'Good. Better to understand,
Goodbody, Light and Dunkel will hand on
Fair copies. And my will is there. My land
Is rich in omnium: fresh research upon
Its fissile properties is ecstatic and
All it requires is cash – they have the data.
Squabble about it at your leisure, later.'

'Plagiarism, bloody plagiarism,' Tim groaned.
'What that word mean?' Yukari asked. 'A poet
Confessed to me in Tangier. He atoned
For a protracted adolescence. So it
Got to the wrong hands, did it? It was loaned
Me for an hour or so. Ah, let it go. It
Summons up something. Now a fresh sonority
Calls. The thugs leave, they recognise authority.'

It was a kind of distant bird-scream. Then
The ancient Byrne was borne in on a litter,
In papal white, light burden for four men,
Old, unbelievably, unfleshly, fitter
For gnomic scrawls from an Egyptian pen
Than life. He bird-eyed with a toothless titter
At the assembly. Then his bird-voice cried
That the door had been locked from the outside.

Hardly a voice, though, from that shrunken wreck.
Ninety? A hundred? Rather a dry reed
Eroded, forced out of a ruined neck.
'I'm he,' it crarked. 'You wretches have no need
To prove identity. Here at my call or beck
All that you seek to demonstrate indeed
Is greed or curiosity. My features
Gleam in a few. The rest are nameless creatures.

'There's a musician son who called me back
To hear by ear what I hear in my head,
Encoded messages. Evil or slack,
Intelligence officials' ears were dead
To brassy information from the black
Nazi interior. Let that discord shed
Generalised light upon a vicious era
And once banned scrawls render the vision clearer.

'You, Brian – Brian is the name? Please go.
You have to work on art's behalf. The rest
Must stay.' He bird-called. Open. Out. One, though,
Shadowily entered. Byrne obscenely pressed
His wrinkles close to Dorothy's. 'I know
You, I think, daughter. I was a paid guest
Of your three mothers. Yes.' He closer peered.
'Are you a witch? Hm, a moustache, a beard.'

Dorothy spat. He howled. Two of his mob,
Making adjustment, seized her. Tim thrust out
A missing-finger hand, then forced a gob
Of pulmonary blood. A porridgy gout
Rusted on Byrne's white cerement. A sob
Of startlement seized all the four. One lout
Screamed as he saw Tim now in repetition,
For it was Tom who had just gained admission.

Unceremoniously upon the floor,
Though littered still, Byrne raised his suppliant claws
To twin sons' hands. The panting groaning four
Howled for an exit, hammered without pause
Upon the adamantine bolted door.
Byrne lay upon a table. 'Ravening maws
Of anthropophagoi grind gutsy lusts.
Appropriate I lie here with the crusts.

'We die, my sons, my daughters. Though my race is
Not widely noted for its efficacity
In the promotion of the greater graces,
In fixing sudden death throes its capacity
Is known, I think. The IRA now faces
A Christmas of quite murderous audacity,
They promise bombs and guns and other gear,
Gifts of a Muslim leader, starting here.

'I've lived a life spurting with brave bravura
Into the *muliebris naturalis*,
Indifferent, *naturalis* as *Natura*.
It's done. You're the part product. Is that Karl, is
That Carlotta? Is that Aqua Pura?
Something. Names go. And rhymes and rhythms. Ah, Lys-
Ander, is it? Hero? Emanations
Of long completed casual copulations.'

(See how the form fades. This is Tomlinson,
Your poetaster, dying not in Berkeley
Square but in a room in Islington.
I cough blood too, thin, thick or lightly, darkly.
Byrne is the killer. See his dim eyes run
On faces that he thinks he knows, as starkly
They range themselves. I have not long to go
But I'll outlast that Swiney Tod, I know.

Names, eh? Oh, there's Crovalis and Novalis,
Pontius, Patroclus, Singapurapura,
Piggery, Pokery, Talis, also Qualis,
And Candelabra, Kish, and Candalura,
Paralysis, Polaris, and Poralis,
De Minimis et Maximis Non Cura
Est est est. Let the bastard snort and snivel,
Audibly fade out, aye, visibly shrivel.)

147

'You might as well go with me. You have done
Nothing to change the world.' 'You evil fool,'
Tom growled, seasonably drunk. 'Here is a son
Who's cracked a wearisome genetic rule.
Feel, fool.' He thrust his full-clothed crotch upon
The father. 'No,' the father yelled, 'No, you'll
Not do that to me.' Tom did what he did
— Martelling on a fancied coffin lid.

'An ithyphallic thrust is not a key,'
Tom said, and pumped his mild voice to a shout,
With perfect phonemes in a cantrip. He
Knew the damned inventory inside out.
TE YESU LL'Ā HA TAE KATA HA TSISI
TSIU HA KABE SITA . . . Had perhaps that tout
Of Brian's, called an agent, stood him lunch? 'I kn-
Ow one thing. Always do your homework, sunshine.'

The homework worked. The door flung open. Four
Black louts first out, a booted octopus
Or pod. The others followed. From the door
They all looked back on Byrne, whose tremulous fuss
At being left alone roused little more
Remorse than Hitler and his succubus
Dying. A rather well rewarded part
For Guinness, though life pays too much for art.

So there they were outside. Tom said: 'You ladies
Go home. I'll follow. Tim and I must quaff
A Christmas Eve potation.' Brisk wind made his
Nose start to glow, Yukari dance. 'He's off
To do his Midnight Mass. So I'm afraid his
Quaffing is out, I'd quite forgotten.' Cough
Not quaff. Tim gave some blood to Davies Street,
A red host that the holy air could eat.

'Well, that's the situation,' Tom explained.
'Fullsize erections, greater than before.
Where does the semen come from? I've obtained
No special message from the prostate. More
Spiritual, surely. Paradise regained.
But Mistress Waters conjured hell. She tore
My bloody bedsheets when I leapt between
The two of them. It quite amused Claudine.'

Crisp bombs erupted in the West, in bookshops
That doubtless sold Dante's *Commedia*,
Provision stores, humble Italian cookshops
That purveyed Dante olive oil (top grade); here
Also a pasta (reaped by that nose-hook?). Shops
Did not concern the IRA. The arcadia
Of posh hotels crashed. In the tube booking hall
Tom asked Tim: 'Have you heard these lines at all?

    'I have raised and poised a fiddle,
    Which, will you lend it ears,
    Will utter music's model –
    The music of the spheres.

    'By God, I think not Purcell
    Nor Arne could match my airs.
    Perfect beyond rehearsal
    My music of the spheres.

    'Not that its virtue's vastness,
    The terror of drift of stars.
    For subtlety and softness
    My music of the spheres.

'The spheres that feed its working,
Their melody swells and soars
In thinking of your marking
My music of the spheres.

'This musing and this fear's
Work of your maiden years.
Why shut longer your ears?
See how the live earth flowers.
The land speaks my intent.
Bear me accompaniment.'

Spring then was needed – the green chirping token
Of sacrifice. Those baby limbs would grow
Into a Hillman's, scourged, finally broken.
Let the logician and the Godman show
The foolishness, but let the word be spoken.
Tim embraced Tom, embarking for Heathrow.
Smiling, Christmas-elated, somewhat sad too,
Blessing the filthy world. Somebody had to.

Ash Wednesday 1993